# Scarface Joe

# Scarface Joe

## PAGE EDWARDS

FOUR WINDS PRESS
New York

Copyright © 1984 by Page Edwards.
All rights reserved. No part of this publication may be reproduced,
stored in a retrieval system, or transmitted, in any form or by any means,
electronic, mechanical, photocopying, recording, or otherwise, without prior
written permission from the Publisher. Published by Four Winds Press,
A Division of Scholastic Inc., 730 Broadway, New York, N.Y. 10003.
Manufactured in the United States of America

10  9  8  7  6  5  4  3  2  1

The text of this book is set in 11 pt. Caledonia.

Library of Congress Cataloging in Publication Data
Edwards, Page.
Scarface Joe.
Summary: Thirteen-year-old Joe spends a summer in
a mining area in Colorado where his relationship with a
girl of another social class gives him both a physical
and emotional scar, which he ultimately comes to
recognize as part of growing up.
[1. Mines and mineral resources—Fiction.  2. Social classes—
Fiction]  I. Title.
PZ7.E2636Sc  1984  [Fic]  83–20667
ISBN 0-590-07899-2

*For* Amy deForest Edwards
*and with deepest gratitude to*
Norma Jean Sawicki

# CHAPTER 1

It was late spring now in New England and Joe Robbins was going to be free from school in only three short weeks. We meet him as he dreams in his social studies class. The warm sun through the bank of windows has set Joe Robbins drifting.

His teacher, Mr. Gadd, began to ask each of his students what his or her plans were after school was let out. Bertie Feather was proud to say that she was going to invent new doughnut recipes for her father to sell to the truckers who came every morning to the Corner Store. Rebecca Majors said that she was going to enter as many roller-skating meets that her mother would drive her to, anywhere in New England. Joe Robbins told the class that he was going to Granite, Colorado.

That news stopped Mr. Gadd and he unrolled the map which hung above the blackboard, but neither he nor Joe, who left his seat, could find Granite.

"It has to be there somewhere," he said to his teacher. "It's between Buena Vista, my dad says, and Leadville on Route 24. It's on the Arkansas River." Joe returned to his desk.

"Well," said Mr. Gadd. "Bill Hymes, what do you have in mind for the summer?"

"I'll be here," said Bill Hymes dully. "I suppose I'll get a tan on Plum Island. Nothing exciting. Then I'll probably go hiking in northern Maine for a month or two and build a boat so my uncle can sail it to England alone."

"I see," said Mr. Gadd, who knew Bill Hymes tended to exaggerate.

Mr. Gadd continued going up and down the aisles.

Joe was going farther away than any of them to a place none of his classmates had ever heard of before.

Then Roy Boland said, "I'm going soaring with my uncle. He builds gliders. Then I'm going windsurfing off Martha's Vineyard."

"All right!" yelled Bill Hymes too loudly, which made everyone in the class burst out laughing, except Joe.

He felt his trip to the West was, suddenly, unimportant. If he had his choice, he realized, he would rather spend the summer with Bill and Roy and maybe they would become good friends.

For now, Joe Robbins lived in a small town in northern Massachusetts, a picture-book town by the sea. Most of the houses had been built years and years ago during the time when the large merchant ships carried textiles from the mills strung along the Merrimack River out to the open sea, and when the China traders docked on the now rotten wharf down on Water Street. Joe had moved to Towlesport in the fall just before school started. It was like no town he had ever seen and he wanted to live there forever. Before that he had lived in Shoshone, Idaho, where he was born; in Grass Valley, California, where he had his tonsils out; in Monticello, Utah, where he tried to run away from home and a neighbor picked him up on the highway; in Farmington, New Mexico; and, in Cedar City, Utah—all of which is a lot of moving for a boy of thirteen.

Joe's father was a mining engineer and was always being relocated to the company's various mining properties in the West. The Amgold Mineral and Smelter Corporation had its headquarters in Boston, which is why Joe and his parents found themselves living on the East Coast after so many years in small mining towns in the mountains and deserts of the West.

For as long as Joe could remember, after just getting used to living in one place, he would be informed by his father that it was time to pack up and move someplace else. The family would move, it seemed to Joe, just when he was beginning to make friends.

He hated the idea of leaving, even for the summer, because he had never made any lasting friends anyplace he had lived so far in his life. Besides, he liked Towlesport and the Middle School—an old red stone building—and his teachers, especially Mr. Gadd. He liked to be able to walk home with his friends from school and to stop at Mr. Feather's Corner Store to buy a fruit-flavored doughnut from Bertie, Mr. Feather's daughter. He liked to live in a town that didn't smell of desert dust or pine needles warmed by the sun, but smelled instead of the sea. He knew that if they left for the summer, they might never come back, and with all his heart he wanted to stay right there not only for the summer but for the rest of his life. A lot could happen in three months' time. In his absence, he felt certain his classmates would forget him and easily continue their lives without him. An entire summer was such a long time that it was quite possible nobody would recognize him even if his parents did bring him back to Towlesport in the fall.

Joe was walking along High Street toward home when Bill Hymes and Roy Boland caught up to him.

"Colorado," said Roy Boland. "How did you get so lucky?"

"It's not luck," Joe said. "I don't want to go. I'll be back by Labor Day. You guys can count on that."

"I'll take your place," said Bill. "You can stay at my house."

"Yeah, I will too," said Roy. "I can't wait to get out of this dump."

"It's not a dump," said Joe. "You should see some of the other towns I've lived in."

"It's a dump to us. Right, Bill? Come on. I'll race you to Boardman Street."

Bill and Roy took off ahead of Joe.

He tried to catch them. "I won't forget what you look like," he called after them, "if you won't forget me." He felt stupid saying that and hoped they hadn't heard him. "Oh, damn it!" he thought, slowing to a walk. "I don't want to go away. Not this summer, not ever." He kicked the sidewalk. "I'll never make any friends if I have to leave all the time."

By himself now, he turned down Market to Mr. Feather's Corner Store. Bertie Feather was already home from school and at work behind the counter. She was only a few months older than Joe, but the apron tied tightly around her waist and the white blouse made her look older. She was not plump either, which was amazing, because she ate all the doughnuts her father didn't sell. Bertie Feather had a real craving for doughnuts.

"You look like you just lost your best friend," she said. "Do you want a jelly or powdered?"

Joe shook his head. "Were Bill and Roy here?"

"Oh, them," said Bertie. "No. And I'm glad. Why?"

"I just thought I'd like to do something with them," said Joe, sitting at the counter.

Bertie opened the display case and picked out a powdered doughnut. "You have nice eyes," she said. "Here. Take it for free. It's too old to sell anyway."

He liked Bertie Feather, but knew that his mother, and his father as well, if he thought about it, wouldn't approve of Bertie, because she had told his mother one time that she was going to quit school as soon as it was legal to go

5

to work full time at the Corner Store. "That's very ambitious," his mother had said to Bertie, but his mother's voice told Joe that she disapproved of the idea. Now as he watched her make a fresh pot of coffee, Joe couldn't help but see how much Bertie enjoyed working in her father's store.

"You really have nice eyes," Bertie said, licking the powdered sugar off her fingers, gazing at him through her dark bangs. "They're so bright."

He felt his face turn red. "So do you," he mumbled.

Joe was fairly certain that Bertie liked him, at least a little bit. But he felt he was never going to find out. He was leaving Towlesport and would never find out about Bertie or anything else there for that matter.

Then Mr. Feather called to Bertie from the back of the store, telling her it was time to get set for the supper crowd.

"See you in school tomorrow, Brown Eyes," she whispered to him, leaning over the steam table.

There was no place else for Joe to go then, so he headed home. He lived just three blocks away, but made the walk take absolutely as long as his patience would allow.

# CHAPTER 2

By the time Joe found himself trudging up the driveway of his house, he had succeeded in forgetting entirely that it was Thursday, his day to mow the lawn after school— even before his homework was done. He had Bertie's smile on his mind, her curves and her concern.

And he continued to think about her as he cut the grass. His mother called from the upstairs bedroom, telling him he had to have the job finished before his father got home, telling him he should have come straight home from school, telling him he looked a mess and was no sight to be seen at supper, telling him that if he didn't change his attitude he was in very deep trouble.

But Joe continued to think of Bertie and tried to do the perfect mowing job he usually did. "Right, Mother. Yes,

7

Mother. Okay, Mother," he said, talking only slightly louder than the rusty hand mower.

To himself, he made a vow. He promised that he would never, not ever, tell her what was the matter. He would not tell her, not even if she asked—which, Joe thought, was not likely. For, to his mother, he was nothing more than hired help, a yard boy. To her, he was a goat that mowed her lawn.

What Joe didn't know is that his father had called from work to say that the family would be leaving for Granite before they thought they would. "It's a possibility that might turn into something," Mr. Robbins had said to Joe's mother, "and, I've agreed to it. I'll handle Joe. Well, I'll do my best."

Joe was finishing the thin strip between the sidewalk and the street in front of the house when his father drove up beside him without even turning into the driveway.

"Leave that for later," said Mr. Robbins. "Get in."

His father was not in an angry mood at all, even though that's all he said. So, Joe left the mower where it was and did what he was told. He kept quiet as they drove through town and down Route 1. His father didn't really say anything except the things he usually said when he had one of his ideas—just wait; I'm looking forward to this; when we get there you'll see; it's a surprise for your mother; I'll need your advice on this.

Joe thought he knew what was happening. His dad said stuff like that to him when they went to Mr. Starkweather's vegetable stand.

So, Joe said the stuff he usually said—school was fine; yeah, it was interesting; well, I traded my raisins; I don't know . . . a banana . . . I don't remember . . . not raisins; Rebecca Majors likes raisins and I like apples, so we trade, so what? We're leaving early, so what? I don't even want to go back to that school anymore. Nobody likes me and it's just an awful place. I don't know, it's just awful. Sure, it will be just great to get out of school a few days early.

Joe had calmed down some by the time they passed the mall and were headed south on Route 1.

"They are expecting us," said Fred Robbins, as he turned into the large and nearly empty parking area for Wally's Used Trailers. The automatic doors opened and Joe's father drove into the mechanics' area where a workman was ready to put a hitch on the car.

In the building, there were three Airstreams, sleek and silver as bullets. And in much less time than it should take to purchase a used, or even a new car, Joe's father had bought a fourteen-foot trailer.

At home, Joe's father suggested that Joe finish the lawn.

"Your mother is not going to like this," said Mr. Robbins. "Not at first anyway."

While Joe finished the strip in front along the sidewalk, he listened to his parents through the open living room window. Their talk had quieted down by the time he tossed the last load of clippings onto the compost pile out back.

"I still don't understand why you needed to buy a

trailer," his mother was saying as Joe came into the kitchen.

"You'll see, you'll see," said Fred Robbins. Then he noticed Joe. "So, here's my partner in crime."

"I have to go wash up," said Joe.

"Oh, don't bother," said Mr. Robbins. "We're just going to work after we eat."

His mother was fuming angry. "I want you to wash your hands before you eat," she told him. She was talking to a pot on the stove. "Your father has some news. We'll talk about it at dinner."

Right, he said to himself, talk. "I'll be right there," he answered.

He tried to sweep away the sinking feeling. He knew that he was going to be told that he had to do something that he didn't want to do. He could tell it by their mood.

"I don't see why you had to go out and buy a trailer," his mother said.

"Just be patient. Wait until Joe is here. You'll see."

"I don't care what you're going to say. It's crazy."

When Joe sat down for dinner, the first thing his father said was that he should clip along the front sidewalk at least every other time he mowed the lawn. As they were eating, his father explained the reason for the trailer.

"Well, a friend of mine," his father said, "a wonderful, crazy inventor I know at Amgold has an idea about gold recovery and I have agreed to try out his idea for him on a small scale, of course, and for a percentage, of course. After all, I'm the engineer."

"And that's it?" Joe's mother said.

**10**

"Well, we have to be out there as soon as we can, before the rivers drop too low and the snow is melted." Then he looked at Joe. "What all of this means for you, young man, is that your last day of school is tomorrow."

Joe felt confused, as if a heavy weight, like an anchor, had been lifted from a murky bottom and put down on his chest.

"Do we have to leave so soon?" he asked.

"It's all arranged," his father said. "I've called your school. I've written a letter for you to take to your home-room teacher tomorrow. What's his name, Gadd. He seems quite nice. Let's start to work on the trailer right after supper and finish it over the weekend and be gone by early Monday. It's best not to travel the turnpikes on the weekends anyway. We need a big drill bit and an airplane propeller. I think the old lathe motor I have in the cellar will give us enough power. Oh, we'll need a couple of fan belts and some brackets. Come on, boy, cheer up. Tomorrow is your last day of school!"

Joe's heart sank.

"Now, dear," his mother said, "it's not the end of the world. If you'd like to you may go to your room. I'm sure your father can work on that trailer alone."

It took his father's arms around him and his soothing, deep voice that echoed now in his own chest to make Joe realize he had to go.

"I don't want to leave, Dad! I don't want to leave. Please, please don't make me." He felt his father release the tight hold he had on him.

"Sure you'll go," his father said, and then hugged Joe

**11**

again. But this time, his father's hug didn't feel the same. It was like hanging onto a dead tree.

"Let's get started on the trailer," his father said. "I must have it ready before we go. I need your help."

# CHAPTER 3

On his way to school the next morning, the sadness he had felt in his dreams gradually left him, then he was angry, then the temptation to throw away the letter to Mr. Gadd which he carried in his pocket left him, too. So, Joe Robbins walked to the Middle School on his last day of the year slamming his right fist into his open left hand, making smacking noises while he swore aloud. "Damn it!" he said each time he hit himself with his fist.

But he knew that he had to go. There was absolutely no way out. Certainly, Joe had considered tearing up his father's letter, but Mr. Gadd knew about it already. He couldn't run away and hide waiting until his parents were gone. He would never stoop so low as to ask Bill or Roy if he could live at their house. There was no way he could live alone. Sure, he could do it, but he'd be found out, that's for certain. No. There was absolutely no way around it. He would give the letter to Mr. Gadd and early Monday morning he'd be gone.

"Damn it!" he said. "Who cares about Granite, Colorado? It's not even on the map."

Joe was crossing Boardman at High and did not realize that Bill and Roy were behind him.

"What's the matter with you?" one of them asked.

Joe touched the letter in his pocket. He wasn't going to tell anyone, but he couldn't help it.

"Are you crazy?" Roy yelled when Joe finished explaining. "All *right*! You're out of this place early!"

Joe stuffed the letter deeper into his pocket.

"Let me have it," said Bill. "I'll change your name to mine and Gadd will never know the difference."

"Yes he would," said Joe. "Just don't forget what I look like."

"That's stupid," said Bill. "How could I forget your ugly face?"

It had rained during the night and at recess a few boys were trying to play basketball around the puddles in the school yard, but most everyone else clustered around Joe because that loudmouth Roy Boland had told them about the letter.

All Joe could say was, "I told you it's a place called Granite. A mining town. I went out with my dad last night and he bought a trailer. We're going to put an airplane propeller in the bathtub that's connected to the old lathe motor that used to belong to my grandfather. And

14

then . . . I don't know . . . we're supposed to get gold."

There was only one person in the school yard who didn't come up to Joe at one time or another during recess. Bertie Feather stood off by herself.

"You should have told me," she said to him.

The bell had rung and they were walking together.

"Do you know what?" Bertie was saying. "Sometimes you stare right at me. How come?"

Quite a few members of Joe and Bertie's class were watching them. The group was huddled together by the outside entrance.

"Tell me," she said again.

For some horrible reason, Joe lost complete control of his ability to whisper or to speak low enough so only Bertie would hear.

"Because you're pretty," came blurting out of his mouth before he could stop himself.

Bertie ducked away from him and Roy and Bill teased him all the way into the classroom, ruffling his hair and making sucking noises with their mouths.

Joe blushed so hard that he thought he might get a nose-bleed. He didn't dare to look over at Bertie. When he finally did, during social studies, she looked away. And Joe thought that she was blushing too.

He wished that today wasn't Friday, his last day of school. All year he had wanted to take Bertie Feather to the movies or something. Now it was too late.

When the bell rang at the end of the day, Joe stayed behind in the classroom to clear out his desk. Mr. Gadd walked toward him.

"I'm sorry to miss the last few days of school," Joe said.

Mr. Gadd put his hand on Joe's shoulder. "No doubt you'll learn more there than you will here. For one, I'll miss you."

"You will?" Joe asked.

"Sure I will," said Mr. Gadd. He had a funny way of hitching up his trousers, which he did now. "Well, you'd better get out of here before the janitor sweeps you into a barrel."

"I was just cleaning out my desk," Joe said.

"Don't you have something for me from your father?" Mr. Gadd asked. "I need it so you will move up next year."

Joe pulled the letter from his pocket.

"Now, you have a good trip," said Mr. Gadd. "Tell us all about it when you get back."

Outside in the school yard, he saw that his classmates were clustered in a group by the basketball net. Joe walked toward them carrying the paper bag which held the contents of his desk—papers, workbooks, old homework, pencils, wads of candy wrappers.

As he approached, his classmates broke up and they all went in different directions. Joe was certain that they were trying to avoid him. Even Bertie Feather looked at him as if he were almost a stranger.

He waved good-bye to her just as she was turning her back so he never knew if she saw him or not.

**16**

# CHAPTER 4

Granite, Colorado, is more than two thousand miles away from Towlesport. It was going to take them five days driving and four nights in motels to get there.

His father drove most of the way, napping for an hour after breakfast and lunch. That's when Joe had a turn in the front, so his father could stretch out on the backseat. His mother was nervous driving the station wagon with the trailer hitched behind.

"It will help if you talk to me, Joe," she said.

He was silent.

His mother looked over at him. Her eyes were soft. "Joe? Come on. Do you know what I do when I feel sad?"

she asked. "I do one of two things. I either take myself back to an earlier time or I try and imagine what lies ahead."

After a while he began to think about what his mother had said and he decided to think about earlier times.

Miles went by. Finally, his mother said, "You can at least tell me about this trailer we're pulling. I don't even know how it works."

Joe did not answer his mother because he was thinking hard now about Roy Boland, about what he and Bill Hymes were doing. He was trying to hear them talking. He wanted to have an imaginary conversation with them.

He couldn't hear anything at first, but at least he could remember them clearly. It was Bertie Feather's voice he heard first in his mind. She didn't say anything he hadn't heard before, but her voice sounded good anyway.

"Mother," Joe said at last, "it makes me feel better to think about home."

But his mother wasn't listening, she was talking to herself. "I watched them take out the beds and the sink and the stove and the refrigerator from that trailer. But, they left the bathtub. They put an airplane propeller in the bathtub. What good is it now?"

Joe's father made a noise that sounded more like a laugh than a snort.

"Joe," said Mrs. Robbins. "Tell me how it works."

Joe left his own thoughts and said, "You crush the rock to a powder and mix it with water and put it in the bathtub. When you turn on the propeller, the sand and all the light stuff gets pushed to the side of the tub and caught in the metal ridges. The gold sinks to the bottom. You pull the plug and out comes gold."

The talk of the gold recovery invention woke up Mr. Robbins. "I couldn't have explained it better myself," he said.

"But will it work?" asked Joe's mother.

"Amgold seems to think it's worth a try," Mr. Robbins said, "that's why we are going to Granite. There are hundreds of old mine dumps in that area. Amgold has leases on most of them."

"Why look for gold in a mine dump?" she asked. "I thought the dumps were waste."

Now that his parents were talking to each other, Joe could go back to what he was doing.

He didn't listen to his father explain that the early miners took out the gold they could see. "Our unit takes out gold you can't see," said Joe's father, "microscopic flakes. The old-timers used sluice boxes and Long Toms that had wooden ridges in them. Water and sand went down square wooden canals and the gold got caught in the ridges because it was too heavy to be washed away. The old-timers found chunks and pieces large enough to see. What they couldn't see is what I'm after."

Mr. Robbins leaned forward and patted Joe on the shoulder. "I mean that's what *we're* after. Right, son?"

Joe pulled himself away from his father's hand.

"Come on now," Mr. Robbins said, "you can't be mad at me all summer. You knew we were going away for the summer. I wouldn't have made us leave this early if we didn't have to. I'm sorry you missed the parties and all that at school. I really am. But your friends will be there when we get back."

The station wagon had no air-conditioning, so halfway through Kansas Joe's father got a block of ice and put it in the footwell in the back. Joe and his mother took turns cooling their feet on it.

"Hey! Dad, this is a great idea," Joe said. He couldn't help himself.

The first mountain they saw was Blanca Peak, rising like an enormous cone out of the Colorado plateau. Then came the Rockies. The peaks looked as if they had been pushed right out of the middle of the plain like a barricade.

"Are we going up there? All the way up there?" he asked, excited now for the first time during the trip.

"Right into the heart of them," said his father, "into the lushest valley you've ever seen."

When his father began to name the mountains and explain the geology, Joe stopped paying attention. He was much more interested in trying to imagine what Roy and Bill would think if they could see such a sight as those mountains.

He thought he heard Bertie ask if there was any place to buy doughnuts way up there. That made Joe burst out laughing.

"What's so funny about Precambrian granite?" snapped his father.

"Oh, nothing," Joe said. "Sorry, Dad. I was thinking about something else."

"Looks like we've got a daydreamer on our hands," said Mr. Robbins. Then he continued to talk about the rock formations.

He was driving now and Joe's mother was next to him with a map on her lap. Joe was in the backseat.

"We couldn't stop at Sand Dunes National Monument, could we?" she asked.

"We might take a day trip after we're settled."

"My lips are chapped," Joe said.

"So are everyone's," said Mr. Robbins.

"It's the air," said his mother. "It's much drier here."

In Poncha Springs, Colorado, they stopped at a gas station that was shaped like an Indian tepee and his father bought them each a tube of Chap Stick. He also bought a canvas water bag which he hung on the front of the trailer.

From Poncha Springs to Granite, Route 24 followed the Arkansas River. In Granite itself, there were maybe a dozen houses scattered on the hillside across the river and two houses, a souvenir shop, and a combination gas station, café, bar, and grocery next to the road. The hotel that used to be next to the antique store was falling down, and the only remaining trace of the old placer mines was the piles of smooth river-bottom stone lining the banks of the river.

During the last part of the trip, Joe remained silent. But he kept pointing wildly out of the window, sliding back and forth across the backseat. He was pretending that his friends were there with him in the backseat and they were all excited. *Look at this,* Joe thought. *Look at that! Where? Right over there.*

Joe's father told him to settle down, but Joe didn't pay any attention to him.

All across the hillside on both sides of the steep valley for as far up as Joe could see were hundreds of abandoned mine dumps, empty shaft houses, and collapsed mine tunnels. *There's one way up there! There's one on a cliff!*

At the Granite Store, they unhitched the trailer and continued up the valley to Leadville. Soon the sagebrush and dry rugged foothills gave way to a beautiful open valley, a flood plain, with ponds scattered everywhere and lush, short grass. Ahead of them, rising from the foothills, were Mount Massive and Mount Elbert. To the southwest rose the Collegiate Range—Princeton, Yale, Columbia, Harvard, and Oxford.

"Well," said Mr. Robbins, "how does everyone like the view?"

Speaking for all of his friends, and smiling to himself, Joe said, "We think it's great, Dad."

"Fred, will you stop for a minute," said his mother. "I feel dizzy."

"So do I," said Joe. The winding road and the altitude were making his ears ring so much he could no longer hear his friends' voices.

"We'll all have to take it easy for a day or two. It's only the altitude," said Mr. Robbins.

They ate lunch in Leadville at the Old Tabor House and made reservations for two nights at the Weld Hotel. While his mother looked in the shops in downtown Leadville, Joe and his father picked up the Jeep that was waiting for them at the Amgold office. They also got the keys to the house and the "shed," which was what the woman in the office called an outhouse.

"Your mother will find out about that soon enough," Mr. Robbins said to Joe as they walked back to the Old Tabor House. "She's not going to like it much."

They both laughed.

A plank bridge crossed the Arkansas River north of Granite. The road cut up behind a hummock and crisscrossed a small stream into a grove of young aspen trees. The house, which was owned and well maintained by Amgold, was small and painted white to match the bark of the aspen trees that grew all around it.

"I must say it looks better than I expected," said Joe's mother.

"Are there any fish in that stream, Dad?" Joe asked.

"No, I doubt it. They'd all be washed down during the snow melt. The Arkansas is your best bet."

"I'm going to use only flies all summer," said Joe. "No worms. No lures. No grasshoppers."

"If you change your mind about worms, try digging near the outhouse. I mean the shed."

"What?" said his mother. "An outhouse? You tricked me, Fred."

"No. I only neglected to mention it," said Mr. Robbins.

"Inside, the house is neat as a pin. We do have to carry our own water, though. And there's no bathroom. We all use the outhouse. The kitchen has a dry sink. No pump."

"Oh, Fred! How could you?"

Joe didn't care about any of that; he cared about fishing and about exploring the crumbling mine dump he saw on the hillside directly above the house. So he only vaguely heard his parents come to a compromise. His mother would reserve a room at the hotel twice a week to bathe. "I'll take the laundry in at the same time," she said, "and have the hotel do it. I'm not a prospector's wife, and I don't intend to live like one."

"Fine," said Mr. Robbins, "and Joe and I will take cowboy showers. I stand on a bench and pour water over his head."

"That's too exhibitionistic for me," she said. "I plan to go to town."

The house had a square tower built on the roof. "Bill Hymes," Joe thought, "if you could see this." Then, he asked, "Can I go up to that old mine, Dad? Please?"

"Later," said his father. "But don't go inside. Never go inside those things unless I'm with you. The timbers are rotten."

On their way around to the back of the house, his father explained how the place had once been a miner's claim. Then Amgold bought the house and all the claims around it. "No one works the claims anymore," his father told them. "But the company thinks someone has been taking a little high-grade ore out of that one up there."

"He must be getting rich," Joe said.

"I doubt it. One man following a single vein, peeling off what he can get, won't get rich. It's not a real operation. It's poaching. And I don't like it."

"Do they know for sure there's someone up there?" Joe asked.

His father looked at him as if he were stupid. "No, but they think they've heard dynamite blasts at night. The only way to get through that rock is to blast and the only sound that's louder than dynamite around here is thunder."

"Then he should work at night during storms," Joe suggested.

His father shook his head.

"Listen, Joe, don't forget this. If someone is up there poaching, he's going to protect his interests even though he's a claim jumper. If you see signs of anyone, you tell me."

"But if he strikes it rich, won't Amgold just take over?"

"We sure would," said his father. "Like a shot."

"So he doesn't have a chance. Does he?"

"You might say that." Mr. Robbins laughed. "You might say he didn't have a chance to begin with."

"Well," said Joe's mother, "shall we go inside?"

Joe felt his father's hand on his shoulder as they followed Mrs. Robbins into the house.

# CHAPTER 5

The stairs from the second floor led up through a trapdoor into a large tower room that had windows on all four sides. That would be Joe's. He could see Granite out of one window far below him, but from the other three sides all he could see was mountains—no houses, no people. In Towlesport they lived right in town and could almost hear people talking in the houses next door. Here there would be only silence and the occasional stirring of the aspen trees that grew next to the house.

"It sure is quiet," Joe said, wandering downstairs. "There's no one here. There's no one here at all."

He looked up at the mountains rising endlessly above him. From where he now sat in the front porch swing, the town of Granite looked like a village on an electric train board. Quiet and dead. There it sat on the bank of the Arkansas River. Dead and empty. Nothing but a string of run-down, falling-down buildings with steep tin roofs.

It was so still he could hear himself breathe.

As beautiful as the mountain sunset was, as blue the sky with a hint of pink Alpine glow, as crisp and clear the air and grass and trees, the silence around him released a vast and painful loneliness in Joe.

"If I cry out," he thought then, "there's no one to hear me. No one at all." And he imagined yelling into the mountains. He imagined the sound of his voice being swallowed by the looming walls of rock.

His mother found him sitting on the porch swing. "Your father thinks we should go into town for dinner," she said.

"I'm ready," Joe said. "Let's go to town."

When they crossed the plank bridge, Joe noticed that upriver there was a deep pool and his spirits lifted somewhat. The water was murky because of the snow melt, but the pool smelled of fish. No matter what, he would use only flies—a Royal Coachman first, then the more natural ones when the water cleared up.

"How are your lips?" his mother asked. "Are they still chapped?"

But Joe did not answer her.

He was trying to think.

A Wooly Worm should be pretty good, he thought, or

a Mosquito. I have to save the Humphy as a last resort, since I just have one of them. Maybe the store in Granite sells trout flies. I need some leaders anyway. Let's see, I've got $4.26.

On the drive up to Leadville and all during dinner at the hotel, his father, who was in an excited frame of mind, announced his plans for the summer. But Joe didn't pay much attention. He was too busy preparing himself to fish that pool. In his mind, Joe could see the entire pool and the exact place where he was going to crouch to make his first cast.

But it was a few days before Joe got his first chance at the pool.

As planned, they spent the first two nights at the Weld Hotel. During the daytime Joe was made to help his mother get settled in the house.

They didn't see too much of Mr. Robbins because he was up at the old Kelly's Bar claim in California Gulch setting up the centrifuge recovery unit. He would come home dirty and tired each night and report to Joe's mother what he had accomplished that day, and it sounded to Joe as if his mother was the boss, not his father.

Joe liked his new room better than the one back East because it had so many windows and especially because of the trapdoor. He painted *Joe's Tower—No Trespassing!* on a chunk of bark and attached it to the door with leather hinges. So whenever he lowered the door, the sign would swing out and warn everyone. Since he was not allowed to put a lock on the door, not even a sliding bolt, he moved a chair on top and sat there when he wanted to be entirely alone. Alone and private.

One afternoon, after they had been there for a week or so, Joe's mother knocked on the sign and called, "Joe, you should be outside." The sign swung back and forth in front of his mother's face. Joe was sitting in a chair directly above her.

"I want to stay here," he said.

She was silent, but he knew she hadn't left.

"Besides," he said at last, "it looks like rain."

"We need milk," said his mother. "Do you want *me* to walk down to the store?"

"Oh, all right!" He put on his shoes and stomped down the stairs and out of the house.

She was waiting for him on the front porch. "You'll need this," she said.

He took the money and wadded it up as he walked, forming the five-dollar bill into a sweaty ball.

There was one other person in the Granite Store aside from the clerk, who had creases in his face that were so deep it looked like his skin had been folded.

A girl stood in front of the magazine rack. She looked to be his age, maybe a couple of years older. She was watching him too, so she couldn't be that much older.

He pulled a package of three tapered leaders off the rack and got the milk and asked the crease-faced clerk if there were any trout flies for sale in his store.

"I just use flies," said Joe. "I mean, I don't know how to fish with anything else."

"Is that a fact?" the man asked.

"Yes," Joe said. "I never learned how to use anything else."

Joe had shopped for fishing flies before and knew he was being tested when the man asked him if he needed a Moth or a Wounded Grasshopper or a Ducktail with the gills clipped way back so that it looked like the ghost of a minnow.

"Humphy," Joe said. "Do you have one?"

From under the counter the crease-faced man brought out a plastic box. "I tied them myself," he said, "last winter."

There in the small compartments of the plastic box were more duplicates of his favorite fly than he had ever seen at one time before.

"A dollar each," said the man.

"Three size sixteens," said Joe.

Meanwhile, the girl had moved away from the magazine rack and was standing next to Joe.

"If you're planning to fish in the river, you won't catch anything," she said. "No one ever fishes there." Her white cowboy hat seemed to glow in the dim light.

Before Joe had a chance to reply, she left the store. She wore jeans and a red cowboy shirt and had long blonde hair. He followed her outside, walking fast to catch up with her. When he passed by, without speaking, she picked up her pace and caught up with him. After passing back and forth a few times, they wound up walking together, fast.

When a brown truck passed, the driver whistled. She raised her hand to wave, then pretended she was adjusting her white hat. They still had not spoken to one another.

Together, they crossed the highway and headed toward the plank bridge. Finally, she said, "I have to wait here for my father. He's on his way up to Leadville and will be by here any minute."

"What color car is it?" he asked her.

"Blue. A blue pickup with a horse trailer. I ride," she said.

She put her hand into the back pocket of her jeans.

"I fish," said Joe.

A truck came sort of loping over the access road from Mount Elbert, baby-buggy-riding on its worn-out shock absorbers.

"Is that your dad?"

"Wrong color blue. We got a turquoise truck. There's no trailer on that one. It could use some work," she said, watching it pass by. "So could ours. Say, where do you live?"

They were at the plank bridge. Joe's tower room was visible from where the two of them stood on the southbound side of the road.

"Up there," Joe said. "You can see my room from here."

"The Amgold house," said the girl. "I heard someone was moving in there."

"It's just for the summer," said Joe.

She had crossed partway over the bridge with him.

"And you're going to fish that? There are definitely no fish there," she said.

Joe looked upriver to the pool.

He was still looking at the quiet water when he heard her boots pounding on the plank bridge.

"Oh, damn! There he is," she said.

She ran across the road toward a beat-up, blue pickup truck pulling a wood-sided horse trailer. The girl—he wished now that he had asked her her name—might have waved her hat to him, or she might have just been fixing her hair or something.

So, Joe waved.

Then he returned his attention to the river. "No fish?" he said, out loud. "What does she know about fishing? Sure looks like fish to me."

He had planned to fish that evening, but it began to rain. The first clap of thunder rumbled down the valley as he was sorting his tackle.

From his tower room, he watched the storm pass down the valley. The thunder began up toward Leadville, passed over Granite, and headed in the direction of Poncha Springs.

Though he noticed that some muffled booming still came from the north long after the storm had passed, Joe didn't pay any attention to the sound.

# CHAPTER 6

Early the next morning, Joe went directly to the pool near the plank bridge and caught a small brook trout on a Royal Coachman. That evening and the next morning he had no luck at all. Rather than try farther downriver in the fast water, he decided to climb the hill and explore the mine dump above the house.

In his fishing basket he had put a candle, matches, a knife, and some string. He went down the road and circled back, climbing up the side of the hill to the old shaft building. What trees and bushes grew there seemed to be clinging to the earth, roots grasping the rock and soil like fingers.

Far up the hillside he found what looked like a slab

cabin built into the mountainside. It had a tin roof, a heavy door, and no windows. Inside, there was a wood floor, a bunk, and tools—ice clamps, shovels, crowbars, two or three picks, a box stove, a funnel, and a rope. The far end of the shaft house was solid rock with a door that swung open exposing the mine shaft itself leading down into the mountain. A small mine car blocked the tunnel entrance. A rush of cold damp air enveloped Joe as he stood gazing into the hole someone had cut into the mountain.

Though he was unable to explain why, Joe felt that someone had been there recently. There was nothing specific that made him think so, except the shaft house was fairly neat. The tools looked put away and not abandoned. The rails that the mine car rested on were not rusty, nor were the points on the picks. Though the bunk had no sheets or blanket on it, the mattress was not rotting. And the door leading into the tunnel was triple thick. Thick enough, Joe thought, to muffle the sound of dynamite.

He closed the outside door and stood for a while in the shaft house, waiting until his eyes became accustomed to the dim light. He felt safe there, and hidden from the world. The air coming out of the tunnel had an acid smell to it—a combination of smoke and rock dust—not the smell that came from an empty cave.

Whittling away the end of the candle he carried, fitting the end into a funnel he found on a shelf, Joe made himself a torch. He squeezed around the mine car at the entrance. Then, a few steps into the tunnel, resting in a niche in the rock wall, he found a box and a half of dynamite and a canister of blasting caps.

Behind him, the outside door to the shaft house creaked. Suddenly, the little room was filled with intense sunlight.

Joe's candle torch went out when he turned.

Standing there on the threshold of the shaft house was the same girl, the same one he had seen a few days before at the Granite Store when he bought the leader and the Humphys. Today she wore a blue cowboy shirt, and that same white hat, which now seemed to glow in the brightness of the sun.

Joe squirmed back around the mine car and squinted at her, trying to make out her features.

"This is private property, you know," she said. "What are you doing here?"

"It's not yours either," said Joe.

For a time, they were at a standoff. Then Joe told her his name and who his father worked for.

"I know," she said before Joe could finish explaining. "Amgold. What do I care?"

"What do you care?" Joe asked. "My dad's company owns this place."

He watched her back out of the entrance to the shaft house and turn heel as if to run away.

As he walked into the sunlight, Joe realized he was still carrying the funnel with the candle. He tossed it behind him and followed her. "What's your name?" he called after her.

"We met," she said. "I'm Mary Cameron."

When she said her name she stopped running and turned to look at him. She reminded him of someone else he knew. It was Bertie Feather, he remembered. She tilted her head the way Bertie did when she talked.

Joe looked at his feet for a rock to kick and found there were plenty of them.

Mary Cameron and Joe watched Joe's right foot kick rocks. After a while, she said, "If you're not going to talk to me, look, I'm leaving." She took off her white hat and shook her head, almost like a horse does. "Hey, I'm over here," she said.

Her frankness was strange. Joe wondered, but he didn't ask, of course, if she was the same way with everyone she met. Mary Cameron seemed to have the ability—Joe never could figure out how, exactly—of being able to tell what was on your mind. If Joe didn't understand, or if he didn't like what she had seen there in his mind, well then, too bad, as far as Mary Cameron was concerned.

"I live up in Stringtown, five miles away," she told him. "There's no one around here who's my age. Let's see if we like each other. If we do, then fine. If we don't, we don't. I can always use a friend. I don't care who your dad works for. Is it a deal?"

Mary Cameron stuck out her hand.

Joe took it.

To be certain, it was an odd way to strike up a friendship, as if friendships are bargains, but Joe felt relieved. The loneliness that had been building up in him ever since he moved to Granite, the secret conversations that he had been having with his friends back home in Towlesport, all became suddenly meaningless to him. He squeezed her hand as hard, almost, as she squeezed his.

"So, it's a deal," said Mary.

"Yes. I don't know. It's a deal," he said.

Though he had released the pressure of his grip, Mary did not let go of Joe's hand. She just stood there holding it for a while looking at him. Then, she said, "Well, I have to go."

"Me too," Joe replied. "I'm going fishing."

He went to the side of the shaft house to get his rod and fishing basket.

"Don't bring that stuff up here," Mary said. "Don't bring anything up here. Somebody may find it."

Then, she was off at a fast run down the hillside toward the road.

She stopped once to call back to him. "I'll meet you at the bridge tomorrow morning!"

As he made his way down the steep hill, he knew that Mary would not be on the road waiting for her father to pick her up, but he looked for her anyway.

Soon, however, the riffle noise from the head of the pool had him captivated and he began to work his way upstream toward the head. "If they're not on the top," his father had told him, "they're on the bottom." Water cascaded over a flat rock about thirty yards ahead of him. He stood in the middle of the river and cast up to it, making the Humphy land in the fast water and drift. Since he stood at the bottom of the pool, the water came up to just below his knees. Though the current was swift, Joe had no trouble with footing or balance, and by standing in the middle of the river he could cast far upstream. "Work all the water," his father had told him. So he began with short roll-casts, covering all the possible places where a trout might be waiting for the Humphy. He roll-cast to the opposite bank, letting the fly drift in the fast current then stripping in the slack. He didn't expect a strike immediately. After all, it was midafternoon and hot. Any sensible trout in that pool, Joe knew, would be deep at the bottom with its head upstream waiting for something worth the effort.

Joe slowly worked the pool. He cast until his forearm was aching. Also, he wished he owned a cowboy hat because he could feel his nose and forehead getting sunburned. He fought against the impatience that comes with fishing. Still, he back-cast too far, making his line crack while the Humphy bounced off a boulder, and the hook's barb snapped. There goes one Humphy.

He switched to a Wooly Worm, but—he should have known it—the fly was too dark for the water, considering the silt from last night's rain.

He heard his father say, "Think before you choose a fly."

"Oh, shut up!" Joe said aloud. How he wished that he would finally learn about such things before he had to try them out. All he was doing now was disturbing one of the few good spots in the river. He should have known better than to have put the Wooly Worm on then.

38

So he moved downriver below the pool and switched back to the Humphy—mainly because he had more of them than he did any other fly. He planned to cast downriver for a while until the pool above him had cooled down from all of his prior thrashing.

At last, a sense of peace came over him, so he turned upriver and cast onto the surface of the pool by the flat rock. The fly did look as if it had been knocked into the current by the wind and was struggling to stay afloat. He stripped in line as the current brought it to him, not reeling in but letting it puddle at his feet.

A large, white thunderhead cloud passed before the sun just as Joe made a second cast into the riffles fifteen or so yards upriver. As if he had been struck by lightning, as if his hand had been taken away from his wrist, a bolt of excitement passed through him and he scrambled over the pebbles through the swift current and, crawling now, set the hook with a firm jerk.

Since the river was swift below them, the trout darted upriver and went deep. The line at Joe's feet disappeared and the reel whirred. Joe slowly moved to the riverbank. At first the thought that this was a dream came over him. As he watched the line move backwards and forwards over the clean surface of the pool, he decided that he was bringing in a pickup truck tire, a horseshoe, an inner tube. The line was that taut. Joe felt the trout (it was a trout!) swimming in a zigzagging course upriver. It had to be a strong one. Small fish, Joe knew, dart downriver and then up. Only the big ones bulldoze to their hiding place; only the old ones try to get home since, after all, they have made it before. Joe was using a one-pound test leader (the one he had bought from the crease-faced clerk at the Granite Store a few days earlier) with a tippet, or extra extension of leader, which allowed the Humphy to float naturally and not be sunk by the line.

"Do not panic!" he heard his father yell at him. He could hear in his mind more instructions from his father. "Keep the tension on the line, bring it in but be ready to release, with tension." His father had all sorts of ideas about how fishing was like living, and Joe was amazed that some of the stuff his father had told him over and over again seemed to be working okay.

The trick was to be firm and gentle. He heard his father say, "If you want to keep her, don't pull too hard." That has always been the saddest part of fishing for Joe, the saddest lesson, but one which has earned him many fish— and he has caught many more after the end of this story. "Don't panic," Joe heard his father tell him. "Don't reel the line, strip it in! Watch for slack and feed it out. Gentle. Gently now. Use some pressure when she tires. Don't rush it. Bring her in slowly. Let her exercise. She'll get tired." The excitement Joe felt then was not the excitement of possible loss, but of action. Nothing else in the world was going on, as far as he was concerned at that moment, but a taut line, tremendous pressure against his wrist, and the glimpses he captured of the trout which seemed to beg for him to get it over with at one moment and then to dart away with the agility of a shark the next.

He must land that trout.

"Keep the pressure on," his father had told him. "But let her think she is free. And don't let her see you. If she sees you, she will fight for her life. Wear her out and bring her in exhausted."

Joe moved farther upriver just across from the flat rock giving her full range of the pool as she raced up and down. Even now, Joe could not, without using too much pressure, get her any closer to him.

"No coaxing," his father had told him. "Firm! Firm and gentle!"

But something was wrong.

His father's stern and commanding voice told him to remain hidden if possible during this phase of fishing. Joe remembered his father describing how hard it is to fish from a boat because the trout becomes frightened when it is brought up close. And now he heard his father say, "If she sees you, she will fight for her life."

When Joe hid behind a boulder, keeping the tension on the line, he found he could strip more line in. The fish was deep now, resting. The direction in which Joe gently guided it, slowly stripping the line in, was the easiest direction for the fish to swim. As the trout found itself approaching the surface, as the water became shallow and the light more intense, it put more strain on the line. Joe released, slowly, a few feet and began the process of retrieving the fish once again. "Wear her out," he heard his father say. "Exhaust her." Time after time, Joe brought the fish just to the surface, just to the small clear water below the rock a few feet from shore. Then the pressure on the line would become too great, and he would let the thrashing fish retreat once again to the depths of the pool.

By the time the fish was ready to be beached, it was swimming toward shore with its head above water, as if seeking air to revive itself, squirming along the pebbled river bottom, wiggling toward Joe as if there were relief there, as if the terrible energy it took to fight the taut line would be reduced by swimming up the bottom of the pool toward the shore.

The dorsal fin was exposed above the surface and the gills expanded violently. "Get your net behind her!"

Holding his rod by its midsection, Joe took up his net and waded into the river. He kept the line taut, he kept the trout's head facing the shore and out of the water, and then in a nearly blind swoop he collected the enormous two-pound brook trout, along with moss clumps and pebbles, and stumbled up the bank away from the river so it would have no chance to escape, and he ran dragging his rod behind him all the way up the road to the house yelling, as if he were yelling for help, "Look what I did! Look what I did!"

# CHAPTER 7

Joe left the house early the next morning and was fishing the river when Mary Cameron called down to him from the plank bridge.

"I've got lunch in this, if we get hungry," she said. "Let's go up to the mine together. No one's there now."

He left his fishing rod under the bridge and climbed the embankment to the highway.

"I caught a fairly big trout yesterday," he said. "Right down there." He pointed at the pool. "I was using that Humphy I bought, with a tippet."

He thought the information might impress her. It didn't.

"I'm going to ride Flame in the Cheyenne Days Parade," she said. There was a tone of challenge in her voice.

Joe did not need to ask her who Flame was. He had watched Mary exercise her palomino up and down the highway. She rode the horse well, but it was too big an animal for her. Joe happened to be afraid of horses.

"You're an okay rider," he said, not wanting to give her too much of a compliment, since she didn't care at all about his fishing. "You have a big horse."

"I'll grow up to Flame," Mary said. "That's what my dad tells me." She smiled. "I am not in competition with my horse. We are learning to understand each other."

"I don't know anything about horses," Joe said. "Besides, I don't have any place to keep one."

Together they climbed the hillside to the mine dump.

There was something about Mary that Joe liked, her secret ways—not sneaky-secret exactly, more careful-secret ways. He had no clue why she liked him, but she must, he decided.

Using his shoulder, Joe pushed open the heavy door to the shaft house.

They stood for a moment facing the door to the mine.

"Have you been down inside a mine before?" she asked him.

He shook his head. "Not recently. I looked inside this one. My dad says these old ones are dangerous and might cave in."

"You've never been in a mine in your life," she said. "I can tell." She took off the green backpack. The candle

Joe had used a few days before, and the funnel, were under the bunk. She picked them up and lit the candle. "Let me tell you a secret," she said. "Promise not to tell?"

Joe promised.

"My dad is working this mine. That's why I know it's safe. He wouldn't go down there otherwise."

"He found gold in there?" Joe asked.

"Of course, silly, how else could he have paid for my horse. Don't tell anyone, especially your father."

"I know," Joe said. "Dad said Amgold would take the mine over if it paid off. Your dad is claim jumping. Isn't he?"

"Well, what Amgold doesn't know won't hurt them. Besides, he doesn't get very much."

"But it's not his property."

"What are you—the police? You make it sound like he's stealing. You promised, remember."

"Okay."

She held out the candle. "Take it. I know my way down there by heart." She had become, suddenly, businesslike.

The flame rose and flickered as they entered the tunnel.

Suddenly, Mary jumped onto the front of a mine car and released the brake. "Give me a push!" she yelled. "I'll race you to the bottom."

He pushed the mine car just enough to get it rolling and watched as it slowly disappeared down the tracks in the tunnel.

"See you at the bottom," she called back to him. Her voice was hollow and made ghostlike by the rock walls surrounding them.

Once again Joe smelled the acid, smokelike dust in the air. The smell he had not understood became clearer to him now. The noise of thunder that had continued after the storm had passed away was now easy to explain. The man who was working this mine, Mary's father, Somebody Cameron, blasted during thunderstorms. The smell was the dynamite smoke and rock dust that had not been absorbed by the walls. After this, he would never forget that smell which is left after dynamite is set off underground.

As Joe slowly descended, the tunnel became cooler. The only light was that which the candle shone onto the tunnel ceiling, so that when he looked back he could see nothing but the two silver rails disappearing behind him. From the moment he entered the tunnel alone, he could hear the mine car clattering ahead of him and Mary laughing and shrieking and urging him to follow her. But soon, she was far ahead lost in blackness, and the isolation of the tunnel closed in on him. The sound of his feet on the tunnel's floor was not like walking outside on a trail, but was dull and close. When he kicked a rock against the steel rails, the noise was not like the bright clang of a hammer on an anvil, but was a deeper sound which was absorbed by the surrounding rock. He passed a number of small tunnels that shot off to either side, but decided to stick to the main tunnel, following the rails.

Mary was far ahead of him now. The isolation of the shaft seemed to close in on him, and Joe felt as if he were locked to nothing more than the light the candle threw onto the ceiling of the tunnel. He could not remember what the entrance to the mine looked like and he did not know where he was going and he could no longer hear Mary's teasing. All he knew was that he was following the rails. All the candle did was to prevent him from stumbling.

Joe was deep inside the mountain when he bumped his leg onto a sharp edge of the mine car, tearing his pants. The end of the mine was an enormous space, as high, it seemed, as the auditorium at school. The rails ended there.

"Mary," he called softly. "Where are you?"

"I'm here," she answered. "Over here. I'm stuck."

On the far wall, he saw her white hat and approached it.

"No, here," she said.

He turned and saw that she was lying on her stomach, trapped under the overturned mine car.

"There was a rock on the rail and the damn thing tipped over on me," she said. "I can't get my foot out."

When he brought the candle closer, Joe saw that he would have to lift up the steel car in order to free her white boot.

He put his shoulder to it. The car wouldn't budge.

"Get that bar over there," she said.

Using the heavy bar as a lever, he lifted the car enough

so that Mary could pull her foot out. She turned over and sat on the mine floor.

"If you can move it," Joe said, "it's probably not broken."

"It's okay," she said. "No worse than falling off a horse."

"Are you sure?" he asked. "Can you walk?"

"I think so." She took a few uncertain steps then fell against him. "I can make it," she said. "If we go slowly."

The mine car lay on its side. "We have to get that thing back up to the entrance or my father will know I've been down here."

So, Joe once again put the bar under the mine car and began to lever it. It rose slowly. Mary helped him push and gradually it tipped back onto the rails.

Joe began to push it up the tunnel. "Are you coming?" he called.

"Keep going. I'm a little slow is all."

Soon, Mary caught up with him and helped him push. Behind them, the candle illuminated their path for a few yards.

"I can do this by myself, if my ankle's not sore."

"Get in," said Joe. "I can push you the rest of the way now. It's not so steep here."

The tunnel made a turn and they were lost in darkness.

They reached a steep section that made Joe feel like he was pushing a roller coaster backwards. He rested a few times, using a rock to keep the mine car from rolling backwards. He was careful to kick the rock aside before moving up the tunnel.

Mary sat inside the mine car. "You're so sweet to do this for me," she told him.

He looked up at her just as the end of the tunnel came in sight and saw her long blonde hair against the sunlight. "Your hat," he said. "You left your hat down there."

If Mary's ankle hurt her now, she didn't show it. She stood straight up in the mine car. "Will you go back for it, Joe? I can't walk back down there."

When Joe got the mine car up to the tunnel entrance, Mary got out.

"I have to clean myself up," she said. "Please. Go back down. Be a sweetheart," she said.

She was entirely unlike all of the other girls he knew. She had a way about her that made him do whatever she wanted, and right now what he wanted to do least of anything in the world was to go back down in that mine alone. But he went anyway.

"I'll unpack our lunch while you're gone," she said. She stood beside the heavy door to the tunnel entrance and watched Joe walk between the rails until he was swallowed by darkness.

It wasn't so bad going down there the second time and it didn't seem quite as far. Even though he didn't have a light, he discovered that all he had to do was follow the tracks of the mine car. Soon enough he made the turn and was able to see the candle still burning just where he had left it in the large cavern at the end of the tunnel. He could even see her white hat reflected by the candlelight, just where she had left it hanging on a drill bit. What Joe didn't see was a hunting knife in another drill hole on the rock face, put there blade-end-out to keep the hole free of dirt so the dynamite would slide in freely. He grabbed the candle, but as he ran for her hat, he tripped over a long steel bar and fell face first against the rock wall.

He felt the blade puncture his skin before he felt the sharp pain and before he heard the sound of metal rubbing against his teeth. It was as if it had happened in slow motion. The puncture, the sting, the sound. His tongue nicked the knife blade and he pulled his head back as if it were a rattlesnake. He could feel the warmth of the blood on his jaw and down his neck.

The tunnel walls were slick with water and slime, but he was not certain enough of his footing so he used them to find his way outside. He was unaware whether he made any sounds as he made his way to the tunnel entrance and he didn't try one way or the other to be brave. He wanted out. He had no other thought than getting out. He forgot about her hat, about the candle.

When he reached the entrance to the mine, he ran out of the shaft house. He did not see Mary wiping the black grease from her boots. He did not hear her calling after him.

He was gone down the hillside, his shirt now stained with blood. His teeth on the right side of his mouth and his tongue were burning. He was too scared to be anything, to want anything, except to get home.

# CHAPTER 8

His mother screamed when Joe came running up to her and she covered her face with her hands.

"I'm bleeding, Mother," he cried. "Please, do something!"

At first, she would not look at his face. Her head made an odd twitching motion. Then she pulled him to her. "Oh, Joe," she said over and over. "Poor, dear Joe."

She made him lie down on the porch while she went for tape and gauze.

The cut was long and deep. Before his mother drove him to the emergency room at the hospital in Buena Vista, she cut long pieces of adhesive tape, taking two triangles out of each piece to shape the strips like butterflies, to hold the skin together. The inside of his mouth was sore and the skin was a flap that felt like a pizza blister. "Don't swallow blood," his mother told him. She handed him a wad of gauze. "Push this on the inside with your tongue."

The cut began at the edge of his lip and ran back to his earlobe. It looked like someone had tried to slice his face in half. There wasn't that much blood, or if there was, Joe didn't worry about it.

Dr. Markson asked him if he had ever been put to sleep before.

"When I had my tonsils out," said Joe.

"Well, I'm going to do that again. I want to stitch that cut carefully."

"Can't you just give him a local?" asked his mother.

"It's best that he's asleep when we do this," the doctor said.

When Joe woke up, his mouth was numb and he had a headache. The first person he saw was his father. "Hello, son. How are you? How do you feel? How did this happen?" Mr. Robbins asked.

Joe could barely hear him. "I'm okay. I feel just fine. My head hurts."

"Leave him alone for now," said Joe's mother.

"I want to know how this happened," said Mr. Robbins. His voice was firm, but gentle.

"I got cut," said Joe.

"Where were you? What were you doing?"

"Fishing," said Joe.

"I don't see how you could get a cut like that fishing," said his father.

"That's what I was doing," said Joe. He looked at his mother.

"Let the boy rest," she said. "After all, he's had forty-two stitches."

"And, he's also going to be scarred for life. I want to know how this happened," said his father.

Joe would tell them nothing more. He would not tell them where he was or what he was doing or who he was with or what implement—knife or nail—had cut him so badly. All he would tell them is that he had an accident while he was fishing.

Not much happened to him while he was in the hospital. He spent the rest of the afternoon there and that night, and was allowed to return to Granite twenty-four hours later.

It was his father who picked him up at the hospital.

A nurse was showing Joe how to replace his bandage. Mr. Robbins looked away just as Dr. Markson entered the room to say good-bye to Joe.

"They always look nasty at first," said Dr. Markson.

"Will he need plastic surgery?" Mr. Robbins asked.

"It's too early to tell," said the doctor. "It's amazing how cuts like that can reduce in time. You'll just have to wait and see."

A nurse wheeled Joe out to the car in a wheelchair only because that was the rule. He had some pills he was supposed to take and some green stuff to put on the tight stitches every time he replaced the gauze. Dr. Markson shook Joe's hand and told him he could "resume normal activities" when he felt like it. Joe liked the doctor because he reminded him of his teacher at home.

On their way back to Granite, his father asked him, "You aren't going to tell me what really happened, are you?"

"I already did," said Joe.

He could not decide whether to tell the truth. If he did, Amgold would learn about the gold mine and take it away from Mary's father. That didn't seem right. After all, Joe thought, Amgold has plenty of other claims. They didn't need to bother Mary's father.

"Well, I can't make you tell me," his father said after Joe had been silent for a while.

They were driving in the Amgold Jeep. It was turquoise blue with the company's name written all over it. His father wore his work clothes and had just come back from California Gulch where he had the gold recovery invention working.

"I want to spend some time with you," his father said.

"If you want," said Joe.

His father did not mention Joe's cut again. Joe spent the next three days either in bed or sitting on the porch swing waiting for the soreness in his cheek to go away. One night before bed, when Joe was putting on a fresh bandage, his father said to him, "I think you better plan to come with me to the dump I've been working early tomorrow morning."

"Fine with me," Joe said.

"Make sure you wear a pair of sturdy boots," said his father.

"I will," said Joe.

"You have a few things to learn about mines and mining."

"I guess I do," said Joe.

Before he went to sleep that night, he heard his mother and father talking downstairs and knew they were talking about him, but he was too tired to listen, too tired really to even care.

He went to sleep that night wondering if Mary's father had put the knife where it was in the bottom of the shaft so that someone would fall on it. He could not believe it was a trap set for intruders in the mine. Then his mind became black from thinking and he fell asleep in his own bed in the tower room with the moon coming in from the window that looked out on the old mine above the house. He fell asleep still wondering.

# CHAPTER 9

Even before he went to sleep, Joe knew how he would be awakened by his father the next morning. And now it was happening and he couldn't do anything about it. Joe pulled his pillow over his head so tight he couldn't breathe. Still he found that his feet were moving over to the edge of the bed.

It's hard to say whether he heard the music first or his father's voice. The sound of the record playing must have gone into the mountains.

"Daylight in the swamps, Joe!" his father called. "It's daylight in the swamps!"

As usual, his father was playing the record that he called his "wake-up record" and the sound of the Swiss horns echoing against his room's walls sounded so close that he almost could hear the horn player's spit in the mouthpiece. The sound came up from the living room, through his parents' room, to his own ears which were covered by the pillow. There was no getting out of it.

"Daylight in the swamps!" his father called, pounding on Joe's wooden sign making it bang against his door. "How's that cut? Be sure to put on a fresh bandage. Breakfast is on the table and be quiet. We don't want to wake your mother."

"I'm up," Joe said. He pounded his heels on the pine boards, trying to make the record needle jump out of the groove, slide like a water skier to one side and go into reject. Joe had no objection to the Swiss horn music. It was clear and beautiful and reminded him of caves filled with ice and odd colors and glimmerings. In fact, he played that same record when he was by himself in the house. It was the timing that Joe didn't like. "I'm coming," he called. "Turn the music down. I'm coming." The side of his face was tight, but didn't hurt.

Every time they went out together early in the morning, like today, his dad brought him from his sleep like that. It was always "daylight in the swamps" and always the Swiss horn. Even when they had deer hunted together and were far from home, sleeping in a cabin, he had been blasted awake by those Swiss horns. The needle was bad and the horns sounded hesitant and wavering, but there they were again: his father's call and those horns. It had always been like that and it would never change.

"I'm awake," he called. "I'm on my way."

The sound of the Swiss horns filled the house now, but his father had stopped calling. There was no way his mother could sleep with the sound of those bright and cheerful horns which called young men into the mountains as flutes call girls to springs.

He would never admit it to anyone, but it was the music that got him out of bed. In the end, it was the music that lifted his sleeping spirit from his pillow and made him rise. There was a sort of march beat to those Swiss horns that demanded that he rise and brush his teeth.

Soon, with a fresh bandage, with heavy boots, with T-shirt, shirt, jacket, and poncho, he sort of tumbled into the kitchen where he found a bowl of cereal and milk in a pitcher and an orange sliced just the way he enjoyed it, in wedges, waiting for him. The orange made the inside of his mouth sting.

His father was nowhere in sight.

Then Joe heard the Jeep start.

His father came into the house and emptied the thermos of its hot water and refilled it with coffee and they were off, together, across the Arkansas River and up Route 24 and past the outskirts of Leadville into California Gulch—a territory that was once lined with miners' tents and pineslab shacks and Long Toms and dredges. It may have been a beehive of activity years ago, but now it was barren. Both sides of the stream were lined with nothing more than the gray and dark blue stream stones left over from the dredges. "That's placer stone," his father told him when he asked what the egg-shaped rocks were.

The vast and flat flood plain below them looked like a large emerald. The mountains rose all around them, but there below it was rich and green and flat. The view of the valley came only in glimpses now as they climbed higher into California Gulch.

Soon they approached a large mine dump which was the color of straw. "That's where the gold is?" Joe asked.

The sunlight on the pile of waste rock made it the color of gold. "We're approaching from underneath, at the bottom," said his father.

The Jeep stopped at the base of the mine dump. On the far side, two workmen sat on a platform built from thick pine boards and railroad ties. A large galvanized water tank, overturned, leaned against the platform.

"So," his father said, "here we are at the Black Jack Mine." Mr. Robbins set the emergency brake. "Get that hat and carbide lamp and come with me."

It was more like a helmet than a hat and the brass lamp fit into a slot in the front. It fit well enough. *Amgold* was written all over the hat, and Joe felt like a walking advertisement for the company.

"What you got there, a new man coming to work, Mr. Robbins?" one of the workmen said, as Joe approached.

His father laughed. "We're going to take a quick peek in the tunnel," he said. "That's my boy."

Together, they walked up the side of the crumbling mine dump to the shaft. The shaft building had caved in years ago from snowpack and neglect and rested off to one side of the entrance into the mountain like a few fallen cards. "When the shaft building goes," his father said, "you get seepage from the head on down. Watch your step in this muck."

Before they entered the tunnel, Joe's father picked up a rusted iron bar that was about four feet long and with it he tested the beams above. Some rotten rock fell. They continued inside a few more feet. Then his father cupped his hand over the silver reflector of Joe's carbide lamp and it spurted to life. After adjusting the water valve, Mr. Robbins did the same for his own lamp and the two of them left daylight behind them. All the while, his father "barred-down" the ceiling of the tunnel watching for hanging walls. "You watch your feet and I'll take care of your head," said his father. "No one has been in this place for years."

Farther down the tunnel they came across a bar that was eight feet long and no more than an inch in diameter. Mr. Robbins used that bar now as they went deeper into the old mine. As they walked and barred-down, his father mumbled to himself. At one point, Mr. Robbins unhooked his carbide lamp and inspected the side of the tunnel. "I see what they did," he said.

Around him Joe could hear the water dripping from above.

"Stand clear!"

Before Joe knew what happened, a hung wall dropped at his father's feet. Joe remembered hearing the tap of the steel bar against the rock overhead. His father's heel bruised his shin. "Stand back!" The sound was muffled and dim. When Joe looked around the bent figure of his father, he saw a mound of rock and mud large enough to fill a ten-ton ore truck. They both leaned against the tunnel wall. "Are you hurt?"

Joe shook his head making the light from his carbide lamp move up and down against the far side of the tunnel wall.

"Move slowly. Try not to disturb the rock."

His father went ahead. Once Joe turned back and in the darkness saw the pile of earth again. It was amazing. It had come down just like that, with no warning.

They were moving topside, quickly now.

As they approached the tunnel entrance a rumbling sound followed them. "It's a cave-in," said his father, calmly. "I wouldn't have taken you in there if I'd known it was that dangerous." His father reached for his hand. "I wanted to show you how to bar-down an old tunnel. That's all I had in mind. I had no idea that the Black Jack would actually cave in."

Even when they were outside in the blazing sunlight, they could hear rock fall from deep inside the tunnel.

"The whole far end of that tunnel was rotten. Anything could have triggered it. Our voices. Our footsteps." They were walking toward the workmen and the trailer, as his father spoke. "Wait until your mother gets wind of this. And she will. I had no idea what it was like in there. The whole place is rotten."

All his father said to the workmen, who were placing the galvanized tub on the platform, was "Nobody's going to get too far in the Black Jack for a time."

"We heard it," one of the workmen replied.

"I'm going to take the boy home," Mr. Robbins said to the men. "He's had quite a shock."

"Oh, I'm all right," said Joe.

"You're going home anyway," said his father.

The Jeep bucked and lurched as they came out of California Gulch so much it seemed that there were no more than three tires—maybe only two sometimes—on the road at once.

When they were back on Route 24 and headed toward Granite, his father asked, "Say, old man, how's that cut of yours? Boy, it's a nasty one."

"It itches," said Joe.

"That means it's starting to heal. I'd stay out of old mines, if I were you," he said, letting the incident drop.

"Does the cave-in mean the end of the Black Jack?" Joe asked.

They were riding on smooth asphalt now heading down.

"Oh." His father took a deep breath. "I suppose not. Some fool will go to the trouble to clean out that tunnel and fill up an air shaft because he's too lazy to take the waste and dump it. I wouldn't be surprised at all if in a few years the whole tunnel is clean and shored with new pine beams and. . ."

They had arrived at the plank bridge.

"Can you walk up from here?" his father asked. "I've got to be there when they set up the tank and I want to get the grinder working."

"See you later, Dad?"

"Say, I'd like another trout for supper, if you can manage."

"I can't promise anything," said Joe.

It was close to noon and way too hot to fish. So, Joe waited until the Jeep was out of sight and headed for the Granite Store. He hoped to see Mary, but if he didn't he had some cash in his pocket and could spend it on something just so it didn't seem like he was hanging around.

From a distance, Joe saw the crease-faced man tilted back in a chair leaning against the side of the store by the gas pumps. The man who tied the trout flies that Joe had caught the big one on was protected by the shade of the store roof, excepting for his boots. There wasn't much road traffic and the buildings in Granite, as usual, looked entirely deserted. In fact, there was no life apparent but for the man with a face like leather snoozing in his tilted chair.

Mary Cameron was nowhere in sight.

Though he didn't change his position in the chair, though Joe hardly saw his eyes open or the slight turn of his head that made his white hair shine in the sunlight, Joe caught the flash in the man's eyes. Then, all of a sudden, there was a pipe in the man's mouth and he was puffing clouds up into the clear blue sky.

"How'd you do?" the man asked, his voice was low and rumbling like someone was scattering gravel over plywood.

"Excuse me?" Joe asked.

"With them Humphys?"

He looked so different sitting outside. There was a calmness about him that the shadows in the store had hidden. He looked like a ghost or a gremlin in the daylight and yet he was not hiding like one. "Well?" he asked.

And before Joe could stop himself he told the entire saga of catching the two-pound trout and the effort it took and just how he did it and how patience was the trick and, oh, it seemed like Joe would never stop talking. And all the time the crease-faced man tilted back and forward in his chair by the store, listening.

"I don't sell them flies to people who don't know how to use them," the man said, looking up at the clouds of smoke he produced from the curved pipe that hardly had a bit left to it because it was chewed down so awful and messy. "Beautiful day," the man said. "We got a breeze from up the valley. It makes it warm. It does." Up went the clouds of pipe smoke. "Real quiet and pleasant."

"Yes, sir," said Joe, ducking under a smoke cloud and entering the Granite Store with more speed than he had intended, leaving the man with the creased face, with ears like first-baseman's gloves.

"That's quite a patch you got on your face," Joe heard the man say as the door closed behind him. The man's voice sounded the way it did, like gravel on wood, because he had ruined his lungs breathing silicates that floated in the stale air of the mine tunnels where he had worked for the best part of his life until he took over managing the store.

Inside, the dim light—in contrast to the bright, hot sun

outside—made it hard to see anything at first except for the soft-drink cooler. He went to it, feeling the cool leakage of refrigeration brush his face like feathers. The long cut on his face was covered with white gauze. He could feel the stitches pull at his flesh slightly when he talked.

He saw her white hat first. She was thumbing the magazines, riffling through one women's magazine after another looking at the clothes and cosmetics that she couldn't afford to buy.

She looked over at him and smiled as if she were embarrassed seeing him. Though they were no more than fifteen feet apart, she waved her fingers at him.

"Hi," Joe said. His hand went up to his cheek to cover the white gauze.

"I have to go," she said.

Joe watched her leave the store.

A few minutes later he left, too. He walked directly across the highway and followed the river up to the plank bridge. He did not look back until he was across the river and halfway up the road to his house. Alone and small, Mary Cameron stood on the highway. She was not waving nor calling to him. She was just standing there looking up the hillside.

# CHAPTER 10

It was weeks before he saw her again.

In the meantime, Joe went to California Gulch with his father to watch the gold recovery machine at work.

How he loved his father during those times. He loved how patient he was when he explained the way things worked. It took his mind off his scar.

The trailer looked entirely different inside from the way it did when they left home. There was a noise, like a blender at low speed, coming from the bathroom and the trailer smelled like the Amgold office, like acid. It made his nose burn.

"I've got the fan in the bathtub going," his father said. "I want you to see how this rig works."

In the center of the small green, kidney-shaped tub was a propeller that had a single wide blade that reminded Joe of the grass trimmer he used at home, except the blade was moving much slower. Next to the tub, where the toilet must have been, was another tank that was filled with floating mud. When Joe's father flipped a switch, it was like he had turned on an enormous blender that was working in slow motion.

"Colloidal suspension," said Mr. Robbins. "Let's give the tub some more food."

He let the blender go for a while before he tilted the contents into the trailer's bathtub. For a while it looked like muck, then the center seemed to become clear.

"Now watch," said Mr. Robbins. "The good stuff stays just where it is and the muck collects on the sides. Just watch. It's the same as the Long Toms and the sluices. The good stuff stays at the bottom. It works. Physics always works. This thing works so well it has paid for our food for the summer and our travel and we'll have something to spare."

"I'm sold," Joe said, thinking about Mary.

Other times he fished. No matter what he did or what he learned she was on his mind. His bandage was off by now and the stitches had been removed.

Dr. Markson in Buena Vista had warned him there would be a swollen pink gash bulging from the side of his face and that it would be the size of a pencil running from the edge of his lip to his ear.

"I'll have this for the rest of my life," Joe said.

"Maybe not," said his mother. "If it doesn't fade a little in time, we'll go see a plastic surgeon."

He was fishing in that same pool, his lucky pool, the place he had pulled out that two-pounder, when he heard Mary calling to him.

"I'm going up to the mine to lie in the sun," Mary called.

At first, he wanted to tell her he couldn't. But her eyes were so brown and shy, like a deer. At first, he wanted to do what common sense told him to do.

But who in this world wants to spend an entire summer hanging around your father's crackpot invention? Who wants to fish for trout day after day in the same pool?

But it was her eyes that did it. She had no real control over them, but they made Joe do what she wanted him to do.

"I've got to go home first," he said.

He was standing next to her now. For the first time, she noticed the mark on Joe's face.

"Just look at your face," she said. "It's all awful. I mean, does it hurt?"

"Not anymore," he said. "It's a little tender is all."

"Let me see."

He turned his face so she could look at it.

She was standing close to him now. "Can I touch it?"

"Sure."

"Oh, look! You can even see the little marks where the stitches were."

"Forty-two stitches," said Joe.

"I think it was my fault," she said. "I'm sorry." Gently, she ran her finger all the way along the scar. "Will it ever go away?"

"No," he said. "The doctor told me it might fade when I get older."

She removed her finger from his cheek now. "I'll see you up there?" she asked. "We're still friends?"

"Yes," said Joe. She looked at him right in the face and didn't seem to notice the mark at all. Only his mother and father did that. Everyone else looked at his scar and their eyes darted away.

At home he found a couple of apples and some cherries to take along. He left his fishing rod on the front porch and began the steep climb to the weathered pine shaft house up the mountain. At the mine, the shaft house was empty and the door to the tunnel entrance was latched from the outside.

"I'm up here," Mary called. "Here behind the building."

Joe looked up to where the sun glistened on the tin roof of the shaft house. Mary Cameron was standing on a level area of grass. She wore her white cowboy hat and a blue bathing suit. "It's really nice up here," she said.

Joe walked the length of the shaft house and climbed farther up the hill to a place that was about the size of the bed of a ten-ton ore truck. In front of him was the peaked tin roof of the shaft house, below he could see his house and Granite and up the highway there was the row of trailers, where Mary lived. The colony of mobile homes was called Stringtown because they were strung along Route 24 in a line leading up to Leadville.

Mary pointed out her father's turquoise-colored pickup parked behind the Granite Store.

"I brought us some fruit," said Joe.

She had a blanket spread out and urged him to take off his shirt and boots. "Roll up your trousers and catch some sun. Or take them off if you want to. Nobody's going to come up here."

Joe pulled up his trouser legs and stretched out on the blanket. Then Mary began to toss cherries at him. "Catch," she said, flipping a cherry underhanded. "No, I mean in your mouth, silly."

The next one landed on his nose. One on his scar. By the time he finally caught one there were cherries all over the blanket and they began to pick them up. Joe had a handful when Mary crawled toward him.

"Here," she said, softly, looking at him with her dark soft eyes.

He took the cherry between his lips, then handed her one the same way.

Joe felt his face getting warm, but Mary did not back away.

"Will you have another, my dear?" she said.

Her breath was sweet against his face.

"After you," he said, "my dear."

Then they stretched on the blanket, turning over every now and then when the sun was too warm. At one point she was on her stomach and he was on his back. She rose to her elbows and with a swift movement of her tongue ran it across his cheek. Her mouth touched his before she pulled it way, just barely touched it.

What happened after that was not quite clear to Joe. He went into a sort of a frenzy with his hands moving everywhere while his mouth searched for hers. He stopped only when he felt her hands on his shoulders pushing him away.

"Wait," is all she said before sitting up. Her back was toward him.

"Why did you do that," Joe asked, touching her shoulder. "Mary, why?"

"I just wanted to," she said, "I'm sorry." Then she reached into the bag and took another piece of fruit. "Come closer," she said. Her lips touched his and passed the warm slippery cherry pit into his mouth. "There," she said. "You must keep that forever."

He removed the cherry pit from his mouth and sat cross-legged covering his cheek with his hand. He closed his eyes to hold back the tears, waiting until the loneliness went away.

No one knows how long they stayed like that—Mary with her back to Joe looking up the river toward Stringtown, and Joe with his hand over his scar. No one knows, because there were just the two of them there and they both had gone away to different worlds.

Joe moved so that his knee touched hers. Then he felt her hand on his trouser cuff. After a while, Mary asked, "Will you kiss me again like that?"

Joe did.

"Be gentle," she said. "Not so fast."

A pit formed in Joe's stomach, but he asked her because he had to. "Will you kiss me again? With your tongue the way you did?"

He felt the smooth warmth of her tongue pass from the corner of his mouth along his scar toward his ear and then back again. She barely touched her lips against his.

"See," she said, "it's not so hard to ask."

"Then, it's not that ugly?" Joe asked.

"No. It's sad. It's not ugly."

When he held her in his arms, he felt as if he had become a part of her. He had never felt that way before, not with anyone.

"I'm sorry," said Mary. "I'm sorry."

She held him and rocked him in her arms. "Poor, Joe. Poor, Joe," she said to him, over and over. "I'm so sorry."

When they walked down the hillside together, Joe kept his hands in his pockets. Between the fingers of his left hand, he could feel the cherry pit.

Joe still has it. Now it's in a leather-covered, oval-shaped box his father gave him. The cherry pit is wrapped in tissue paper, like you wrap a lost tooth. The oval box is in the top right drawer of the blue antique bureau they brought back from Granite that summer.

The pit is dry now and cracked, not smooth and slippery as it was when he felt it in his pocket after leaving Mary Cameron that afternoon.

His mother was on the porch when he came down the hillside.

"How was fishing?" she asked him.

"Didn't fish," he said. "I was with Mary."

His mother was in the swing and his fishing rod was right behind her leaning against the house where he had left it.

"Who is Mary?" she asked. "I didn't know you had found yourself a friend."

He answered a few questions about Mary, such as where she lived and what she was interested in. All the time, Joe just wanted to get past his mother so he could go up to his room.

"I'm not saying you shouldn't be friends," his mother was saying, "but you must remember she is quite a bit older than you are."

"I don't care," he said. "So what if she is older!"

Upstairs in his tower room, with the trapdoor closed and a chair over it, he took the cherry pit out of his pocket and moistened it. When he moved it gently over his scar the way Mary's tongue had, he could feel her hands on his shoulders and her breath against his face.

# CHAPTER 11

That night, when Joe was almost asleep, his father came up to the tower room and sat on his bed. "Did I wake you?"

"Sort of," said Joe.

"There's something your mother and I both feel that I must tell you," Mr. Robbins said, putting his hand on Joe's shoulder. "It's difficult for me to tell you this. I don't want to hurt you. When I hurt you, it hurts me just as much."

"I want to tell you something, too," said Joe. "Or ask."

"Just be quiet." His father paused, and a coldness came into the room that made Joe sit up in his bed. "You have been seeing quite a bit of Mary Cameron, haven't you?"

"Yes. She's my friend."

"She was your friend," said his father. "Let me explain this if I can." His father moved to sit on a chair. "Mary," he said, "is Max Cameron's daughter."

Joe started to say something.

"Now, let me finish. We at the company, at Amgold, have reason to believe that it is Max Cameron who is claim jumping in that old mine up above the house. And, the company feels that we can't let that sort of activity continue."

"What does it have to do with me?" asked Joe. "I don't know Max Cameron. I don't even know what he looks like. Mary is my friend. That's all I care about."

"Look, Joe. Don't tell me you don't know Max Cameron. Also, you know the kind of man he is. I don't want you getting mixed up with people like that. He's nothing more than the owner of a rundown store in a broken-down town who makes some extra money jumping my company's claims. You don't want to get mixed up in that. Besides, if he ever struck gold, he'd hoard it and take himself and his daughter out of here. It's not you, Joe. They aren't our kind of people. Those Camerons."

"What do you mean he owns the store?" Joe asked.

"That man in the Granite Store is Mary's father. I thought you knew that."

Just to make sure he wasn't hearing things, Joe asked, "You mean that the crease-faced man who sold me those Humphys that he tied is Mary's father? Is that who you mean?"

"Yes. That's the man. I thought you knew it all the time."

"I didn't. She never told me," Joe said. "And he never told me."

"Well, I'm telling you right now, and I would prefer it if you would not spend so much time with his daughter."

Joe tried in vain to protest.

"All you'll do is wind up getting hurt again," said his father. "I know how you got that awful gash on your face and I know why you got it. Cameron left that mine booby-trapped, just as sure as day. Those people aren't your kind of friends, Joe. They are only looking out for themselves. I wouldn't be surprised if that daughter of his didn't work with him in that mine as his partner. She knew that knife was there, just as sure as her father put it there."

"I don't believe you," he said. "It was an accident." He was on the verge of tears. He couldn't control the way his face moved and he couldn't control the sense he had that it was all a lie. "I don't believe you," he said again.

"I know what goes on around here," said his father. "That's partly what I get paid for."

"I still don't."

"Now, don't be impolite to her or snub her or anything. Let her down easy, or she will suspect you know. But, I would prefer it if you stopped considering her your friend. I know you'll do the best you can."

It was worse than a bad dream.

"I have to brush my teeth," said Joe, trying to think of a way to escape.

"Just remember what I said." Before his father left Joe's room, he added, "We may not catch him, but we are pretty certain who he is."

Joe had kept his promise to Mary. He hadn't told his parents anything at all about the mine or the dynamite or anything. He couldn't believe that it was really Mary's fault that he had been cut that way, but now suspicion entered his mind. Possibly Mary did know about the knife. Maybe she and her father could work the mine without being discovered. But that was impossible. Mary is not like that, he thought. Mary would never do that. Not Mary.

Before he went to sleep, he decided that he would ask her. She would tell him the truth. His father didn't know anything. His father was trying to bluff information out of him. His father was interested only in company property. His father didn't care about anything but Amgold property. His father didn't care about anything.

He and Mary had agreed to meet up at the mine the next day when the sun was high, around eleven, he would find out then. No matter what his father "preferred" there was no way he would not meet her. Besides, his father had asked him to let her down gently.

The thunderstorm that passed down the valley early the next morning did not help Joe's sleeping. It was still raining when he finally got himself out of bed. There would be no picnic on the blanket up at the mine today, that was certain. He stayed in bed listening to the rain on the tin roof above him until he heard his father leave for work.

His mother told him, "She must be a nice girl, or you wouldn't like her. Your father was upset last night. Just don't set your heart on her. You might get hurt."

"Yes, Mother," said Joe. So his mother was on his side. "I'm going out."

"It's raining," she said. "Your father's left already."

"I don't care. I'm going out."

The yellow rain slicker he wore was small for him, but the hat fit and so did the high yellow boots, if he didn't wear shoes. Joe slogged down the road to the plank bridge. At the point where he usually turned upriver to climb the mountainside for the old mine dump, he looked up and saw the thunderheads were low enough to obscure everything above about fifty feet. She wouldn't be up there. She might be at her trailer in Stringtown, but he couldn't go there. All he knew was that he wanted to stay away from home as long as he could.

Thunder sounded around him then. There wasn't much rain. There was no lightning. Still, three short blasts of thunder sounded.

The Granite Store was closed, so was the gas station. But Joe kept on walking down Route 24 for a while, just to get out of the house. He didn't care where he went. He just kept walking.

It started to rain again, but he was protected well enough.

Then he turned around and came back up the road. He hadn't gone anywhere, really, there was no place to go from Granite on foot. It was about eleven when he passed the gas station again. The rain was falling straight down. It didn't fall that way at home in Towlesport, it always slanted because of the wind. There was no wind here, only rain coming straight down on his yellow hat. He wasn't especially cold or especially wet; he was just walking, that's all. There was more thunder now that sounded like oil drums being rolled down the mountain. He passed by the Granite Store. It was still closed.

Joe had just about decided to go home when he saw someone in a red poncho in front of the pay phone up by the falling-down hotel. He didn't know for certain it was Mary until he was only yards away from her. When she recognized him, she hung up the phone and, before greeting him or getting her dime back or anything, began to giggle. Her laughter was quick and bright and carefree and seemed to make the storm clouds lift.

"Do you know that for a minute I thought you were Paddington Bear," she said. "Where did you get that rain suit?"

"It's a nor'easter," said Joe, "what the fishermen wear at home."

"Well, it's real cute," she said.

They walked together along the highway.

"Who were you calling?" he asked.

"You, of course."

"I don't believe you," he said.

"Well, it's your tough luck if you don't."

They crossed the plank bridge. She wasn't going to leave him, he realized.

"I feel protected by rain," said Mary Cameron. "I love this poncho. No one knows who I am in it."

Joe was quiet for a while. Then he asked her, "Is that your father who is in the store all the time?"

She would never lie to him. "Why do you think I'm there all of the time? You must have seen his truck out back. Of course he's my father."

"He wasn't there today," Joe said.

"He didn't open the store today. He never does. No one comes by when it's stormy," she said.

"He must be tying flies, then," said Joe. "I hope he's tying Humphys."

Mary was quiet.

"He's not," she said, finally. "You know where he is."

They were approaching his house now. Joe had no idea how it had happened, but they were walking together and had crossed the bridge and were suddenly there. As they got closer to the house, Joe decided that he would show his mother just how great Mary was. If his mother only knew her, then she would like her as much as he did. So he didn't stop.

Mary lost her footing climbing up the last steep part and Joe took her hand. He did not let go of it until they were on the front porch. If the truth be told, he wouldn't let go of her hand, though she sort of pulled and tried to make him.

"Are you sure this is all right?" Mary asked him in a whisper.

"It's my house as much as theirs," he said.

His mother had seen them coming up the drive and had seen that they were holding hands and also had recognized whom Joe was with. She met them on the porch. "I'll make hot chocolate," she called. "Bring your friend along with you."

Thunder sounded in the hills again.

"See," said Joe. "It's okay."

Mary seemed to know what Joe was thinking. "It's these boots," she said. She made her voice get louder, "I always slip on hills in these boots. Thanks for helping me up," she said, shaking his hand away.

His mother watched them stop holding hands. "Why don't you and your friend leave your rain things on the porch?" she suggested. "It isn't much of a day for fishing, is it, or a picnic? Well, come along inside and get dry. It's almost lunchtime."

Mary stripped off her poncho and was out of sight even before Joe had one boot off.

"Say, this is a real nice place," Mary was saying. "We live in a pretty neat trailer down in Stringtown. But it's not like this. My dad's not too particular where he lives. Anyway, a trailer is real easy to clean up."

"So, you do the housework?" his mother asked.

"Sure," said Mary. "Dad's not home much. The store takes a lot of time. And he's on the Colorado Mounted Patrol. He's planning to ride in the Cheyenne Days Parade this year. When I'm seventeen, I get to try out for Queen."

"Is your father at the store now?" his mother asked.

"Oh, he doesn't open the store when it's thundering and rainy," said Mary. "It's not worth it." Mary paused. "That's what he says."

"I see," said Joe's mother. "Then, he's doing something else."

"What do you mean?" asked Mary.

"Well, what does your mother think about all of this?"

"She don't know," said Mary. "She's not living with us right now. She's working in Reno."

"That's very nice," said Joe's mother. "Joe, why don't you take your friend out to the pump and wash your hands while I get lunch on the table."

They were on their way out into the yard where the pump was when they heard Joe's mother call, "Wait just a minute, Joe. I'd like a word with you."

The storm had passed down the valley. The sun had brought with it a wind from up the valley. The storm was over, but then came another blast of what sounded like thunder from the north.

"You know what your father said about the girl," his mother said.

"Yes."

"I can't very well send her away. But let's not have this happen again."

Joe took Mary's place at the pump and by the time he was back in the house Mary was chatting away with his mother. "You know, Mrs. Robbins, you've fixed this place up real nice. We don't live so good as this. I like it here."

"Why don't you show Mary around, Joe," Mrs. Robbins said. "I'll call you for lunch."

82

It seemed to Joe that Mary was more energetic and excited at that moment than he had ever seen her before. When they were alone, she was much kinder, it seemed, and softer. Now, with his mother there, she was one regular chatterbox of a girl.

He showed her the downstairs, then they went up to the second floor.

"Your mother is quite nice," said Mary. "Real nice, really."

"Well, she's acting a little weird today," said Joe. "She's all right, I guess."

"This house is huge. I want to see all of it."

She stopped at the stairs leading up to Joe's room to read the sign.

"You mean, your room is up there?"

Joe passed her on the stairs and pushed open his trapdoor.

"What a room! It's enormous!" said Mary. She looked out of each window and Joe showed her how he moved the chair over the trapdoor to be private. From one of the windows, Mary observed that she could see the shaft house and the mine dump where they met.

Together they devised a plan. Rather than her calling him on the phone or their meeting by chance at the Granite Store, why not signal to each other. It was decided that when Mary was up at the mine she would spread out a white towel. If Joe was coming up there, he would pull down his window shade.

"Why do we have to do that?" Joe asked, knowing perfectly well why they had to.

"I get the feeling your mother doesn't like me too much," said Mary. "She's just too nice."

Then Joe heard a quiet knocking on the trapdoor. "It's time for lunch," his mother called.

Neither of them knew how long she had been standing there or if she had heard them. If Joe's mother was suspicious, she didn't mention it to them during lunch.

They ate lunch on the porch. The rain had stopped and the air was sparkling clear, as it always is after a rain in the high mountains. All that was left of the rainstorm now were wisps and spirals of clouds that clung like streamers of smoke to the peaks across the valley. The sky above them was clear and blue as if the storm had never happened. The sagebrush on the hillside above the house was a deep green and the rocks glistened. A muffled sound of thunder came from up the valley, then it was quiet except for the creaking of the swing.

After a while, Joe said, "That noise was your father in the mine, wasn't it?"

"Don't talk about it here," she said. "Somebody might find out."

Just then Joe's mother came out onto the porch. "Joe," she said, "I'd like you to help me in the yard this afternoon. I think it's time that Mary went home."

"I was just on my way," Mary said, brightly. "I've just got to find my hat."

"Here it is, dear," said Mrs. Robbins, handing it to her.

"Well," said Mary, "I'm in a rush. Thanks for lunch, Mrs. Robbins. See you, Joe," she said.

When Mary was gone, his mother told Joe that she would not report his meeting Mary to his father. "You've had your last chance, young man," she said. "She seems like a nice girl, but remember what your father said."

Joe put up a fight, just to seem convincing. He knew he would see Mary again.

"And furthermore," his mother said, "I don't want you making so many trips to the Granite Store. If you happen to see the girl, you must be polite, of course, but no more than that. Do you understand? Joe, are you listening to me?"

"Right, Mother," said Joe.

"Well now," said his mother, "it's turned into a beautiful day and you can find something to do or you can help me weed the strawberry bed."

"I think I'll find something to do," said Joe.

"You could go fishing," she said. "That fishing pole has been there for weeks. It's gathering cobwebs."

"It's a rod, not a pole."

Nothing was going to keep him from seeing Mary. It had been twenty-four hours since they had kissed. As Joe listened to the sound of his mother's voice, but not to what she said, Joe thought of Mary. He thought of how she would be when he saw her the next day. She would be up in the soft grassy spot above the mine tunnel with the sun filtering through the aspen leaves making heart-shaped shadows on her skin. She would be wearing her pink shorts, or maybe her white-and-green striped ones. If she were lying on her stomach, her back would be bare.

If she were lying on her back, she would have only a folded towel over her front. He could see her, as clear as the sky, waiting, waiting for him. No one in this world had ever waited for him like that before.

"All right! I'm going!" Joe said to his mother. "I'm going!"

Nothing in this world, no one, could stop him. No matter what. He would always answer Mary Cameron's signal.

# CHAPTER 12

It was now early August and there were just a few weeks left. At that time of year in Granite, the hillside is ablaze with wildflowers—Indian paintbrush, columbine, wild geranium, and many other flowers that Joe had not learned the names of yet. The Arkansas River was much lower now and was running much clearer, though it never does run clear like a high mountain stream because of the silt. The fishing at that time was both easier and more difficult. He could hit the pools with his Humphy and his Wooly Worm, but did best in the riffles with more colorful flies. He was bringing home so many trout that his mother asked him to stop trying to get his limit of ten every day and to bring home only what they needed to eat. His father would eat trout three times a day, but his mother had grown tired of them. And Joe knew no one to give them away to because he had stopped going away from the house. He spent his time in his room looking up at the mine dump or on the stretch of river near the plank bridge. In all the days that passed, he did not let himself lose sight of the mine dump. To keep himself occupied, he split wood for the stove and learned to identify wildflowers. He went so far as to make a flower press so he could collect and label the ones he could identify from a book on western flowers.

He wasn't that unhappy. He kept himself busy and kept his thoughts to himself.

He was on his way down the road to fish one morning and looked up to the mine dump. The blaze of white on the gold-colored rock confused him at first. It seemed odd, and it took Joe a few minutes to understand that it was Mary's towel up there spread on the top of the crumbling mine dump signaling him.

He turned and ran back up to the house and up to his room.

He had the shade in the window pulled down so far he could hardly see out from under it, waiting for Mary to answer his signal by taking the towel away.

"What are you doing?" his mother called. "I thought you went fishing."

"I forgot my flies," Joe called, glad he had remembered to put the chair over the trapdoor.

The towel was gone when he looked outside again and he raised the window shade.

Joe does not remember running down the road to the

river that morning where he hid his fishing rod under the plank bridge. The thought of seeing her had flooded over him. He scrambled up the hillside and could have found their special place if he were blind. He could be on the end of a fishing line and she could be reeling him up to her. He didn't care if he was an old shoe or an old tire being reeled in, nothing mattered to him then, nothing mattered but Mary. He could not feel his feet on the ground as he hurried up to her, up to their private place, that soft bed of grass surrounded by aspen trees that Mary called "The Tub."

He was completely out of breath when he got to her and even now he can hardly recall everything that happened that morning. He does remember that he called her name and that he found her sitting up holding the folded white towel to her front.

"Rub-a-dub-dub," she said, "welcome back home to our tub."

Then she rolled toward him.

"You may kiss me," she said, reaching out for him. "Right now!"

It was awkward at first and then wonderful and they held each other for what seemed like hours.

After a while, Joe whispered to her, "You know we could get some chairs and a wood stove and a lamp and get married and live up here."

"Oh," Mary replied, as if she had been awakened from a dream.

"And some pots and pans and canned stuff, and I could mine for gold."

She seemed dazed. She sat up and turned her back to him.

"I mean we could live in the shaft house. We could, you and I."

She began to button Joe's shirt.

"That's impossible," she said. "This is my father's mine."

"His?" Joe asked. "This place belongs to Amgold."

"Don't tell. Can you keep a promise?"

She ran her finger along his cheek.

"I never told how I got this scar," he said. "And I never will."

"We can't live here," she said. "We can't live anywhere."

"I don't understand."

"I must stay with my father," she said. "He doesn't have anyone else. He doesn't. I know he doesn't."

"What about me?"

"You're going to leave here soon and go back to your home. I'll never see you again. That's just the way it is."

"How do you know?"

"Look, Joe. Forget it. I just know, that's all. Don't make me talk about it. Believe me. I know."

He wanted to hold her then, but she didn't want to be held anymore. It seemed that she wanted to cry, but would not let herself cry. So, she sat there waiting for the sadness to go away.

That was one of the wonderful qualities about Mary that Joe would never forget for as long as he lived. When

Mary Cameron was sad, she didn't go off somewhere to pout. That afternoon, Joe had no desire to be anywhere but with her, and she let him stay there. Who knows what Mary was thinking, while they sat in silence. Joe was trying to recover from his broken dream of living with her in the shaft house and mining for gold. Yet, after a time, they began to talk about other things and laughed some, and it was as if the sadness hadn't happened at all. She was amazing that way, Mary. She was a rock-hard realist, Mary Cameron was, and one of the few he would ever meet in his life.

That afternoon they talked about all sorts of things. They talked about how Mary's father could mine for gold without anyone knowing he did it—blasting during thunderstorms and putting the waste rock in old tunnels and air shafts in the huge vacant mine. They talked about her life in the trailer in Stringtown, about her father's temper and why it was so harsh, and how bad tempers come from hard circumstances in life more than anything else. "Your father can afford to be kind," she told him. "Mine doesn't have enough money."

She wasn't the chatterbox she had been before, and Joe saw that she did know much more than he did. Not that she was older, the way his mother claimed, but that she was more experienced. She was able to look ahead, to see.

"I like you," she told Joe. "I really like you, no matter what. But you'll go away."

"How do you know?"

"Ask yourself. Are you going to stay here?"

"I could."

"That's the difference, you see. I have to stay here." She didn't sound sad saying that, as Joe expected she might be. Mary Cameron was a realist, but she liked him anyway. Then, she told him, "If my father has to get out of the mine down there, he can't pay for my horse. I don't know what I would do if I lost Flame. He would also have to sell the store, and he likes it there, even though there aren't many customers."

As she spoke, she ran her finger over the scar on his face. She touched it as if she were curious about it, not trying to heal it. Mary had plenty of scars of her own, even if they did not show.

The sun was over Mount Massive by the time they walked back down the hillside and parted. The last thing she said to him was that he must promise to tell no one that her father was working the Amgold claim up on the hillside. "He's not mean, my father," Mary said, "but he'd kill me if he knew I'd told anyone. You're the only person I've ever told. Don't be a rat."

"I'm not," said Joe. "When will you put your towel out for me?"

"When I can," she said. "I'm pretty busy these days. And I've got Flame to take care of. I don't know. My dad's sort of watching me. I've got to go now."

Joe was almost at the house when he remembered that he had left his fishing rod hidden under the plank bridge. So he went back down to get it. Trout were rising in his favorite pool, but he didn't even bother to cast the Mosquito he had used with good luck earlier in the day, or was it the day before, he couldn't remember. He had lost something up at the old mine that afternoon, something he didn't understand. She seemed so different. It was as if she was spending time with him to be polite. She hadn't acted that way at first, but now she seemed so different. She hadn't said anything, it was just a mood. He couldn't figure it out. It was as if she had told him something that he didn't want to hear without actually telling him anything in words.

Maybe she did have something to tell him, but maybe even the old chatterbox in her didn't have the words to say it.

Anyway, the porch light that Joe saw when he came home that evening was just about the coldest and harshest light he had ever seen in his life. It made him think hard about what he didn't know.

# CHAPTER 13

The prospect of spending an entire day without seeing Mary was not a pleasant one. Joe tied on one of Max Cameron's Humphys and cast into the pool by the plank bridge. He fished halfheartedly and got little thrill from the two rainbow trout he caught.

The sadness that filled him was like nothing he had ever felt before. He had no reason to believe that she had stopped liking him, she hadn't said that. Still it was as if an enormous rock wall had come between them. She had sent him away and he knew that she had not wanted to do that, he knew it. If only he could tell her now what a comfort she was to him; how his world changed when she laughed—even when she laughed at him and called him

"Scarface Joe" to make it so he didn't feel so badly about the mark on his face. He told himself that Mary had not changed her feelings about him, that it was his father and her father who had made her act toward him as she did. It wasn't the way he looked, it wasn't the way he was, it was someone else's doing. It was other people who made life confusing, not him, not Mary.

Joe was cleaning the fish on the riverbank when his father's Jeep rumbled onto the plank bridge. Mr. Robbins honked and motioned for Joe to come and get in.

"I got two small rainbows is all so far," said Joe.

But from the coolness of his father's response, Joe knew that not even a fifteen-inch brown trout would have made any impression on his father then.

"Come inside, and go into the living room," said his father. "I want your mother in on this too."

Joe sat in the straight-backed chair while his father paced the room. They were silent for a long time. His mother stood in the doorway. It seemed like hours passed before his father decided what he was going to say to them.

"Now, Joe," said his father. "Tell me about that old mine up on the hill."

"What about it?"

"Have you been going inside?" Mr. Robbins asked.

Joe hesitated. "Just once," he said. "A long time ago, before you took me inside the Black Jack. I got scared when all that rock came down."

"Does anybody else go in there?"

Now, he had to lie. He had promised Mary. "No. Not that I know of."

"Well then, tell me about this friend of yours. This Mary Cameron. What's going on? You've been seen up there."

"Nothing," he said. "I don't think she wants to see me anymore."

"You're telling me that you two don't go into that mine together? Is that right?"

"Yes," said Joe. "We stay outside."

"Would you like to continue seeing her?"

"Yes."

His father could be stern and persistent at times. It wasn't the questions he asked Joe but the way he asked them, as if he, Joe, were one of his father's scientific problems that had to be figured out. It made him feel ugly and useless.

"We don't do anything wrong! She won't let me!" Then, he said, not from shame, but from frustration, "There. Now you know. And you don't care."

His father shook his head.

"Fred," said Joe's mother, softly. "It's only a crush. That's all. You can't control Joe's feelings, after all."

He wanted to kill them both. It was not a crush. At that moment he had never loved anyone more than he loved Mary Cameron.

"Besides," his mother said, "she's quite a nice girl. She may be a little old for him, but I don't see anything wrong if he has her for a friend."

His father was silent.

In her quiet and firm way, Joe's mother said, "Fred, I think you should at least meet the girl. She's sweet, really."

"I'd be glad to," said his father, roughly. "Invite the girl for dinner. Tonight. Why not tonight? Let's get it over with."

"Now, Fred."

"All right," said his father, calming down.

It was amazing the influence his mother had over him.

"So, I'll go and find Cameron. He's at the store now. I saw his truck there when I went by."

"Oh, Dad. You will?" Joe tried not to sound too relieved.

"Sure," said his father. "I guess I'd better have a look at her."

Throughout lunch his father talked on and on, but Joe did not hear a word of it. Mr. Robbins talked about how well his gold recovery method worked on a small scale, he talked about the possibility of using wind to separate gold the way the old-timers used water, he talked about the possibility of rocketing shipments of high-grade into space where gravity control is more precise. Most of the time Joe thought things like that were terrific, but today Mary Cameron was on his mind.

"Joe," his mother said. "At least try and eat something. It's a long time until dinner."

He could do little more than nod and wave when his father went back to work, for his mouth was full of food he could not taste.

"Why don't you try and catch a few more trout, and I'll

fry them for dinner," his mother said.

Then he looked at her. "Thanks, Mom," he said.

He fished hard that afternoon, too hard perhaps, trying to bring home enough trout for Mary. He changed his fly ten or twelve times. He used a Wooly Worm, a Renegade—even a Royal Coachman. Nothing worked. Not a rise. Not a strike. Nothing all afternoon. His heart was too much in his fishing. Yet he was casting well, so the fly hit the water before the tippet and line. He tried to be patient, to remain calm, to retain his concentration on what was going on under the surface. Still he didn't get a bite.

Mary would understand. He would tell her how well he fished, how he had thought about her the entire time, how he was fishing for her that evening, fishing to bring home dinner to her, but he just didn't. Mary would understand that.

# CHAPTER 14

Perhaps it was a mistake that Joe went to get Mary by himself. Late that afternoon, his father called to say that Max Cameron would allow his daughter to come up to the Amgold house for dinner. When Mr. Robbins offered to drive Joe to Stringtown to pick up Mary, Joe told his father that he would rather walk. It was probably a mistake.

As it was, Joe arrived alone and knocked on Mary's trailer. He had a hard time finding her trailer and wouldn't have found it at all if he hadn't recognized Flame corralled out back.

Joe knocked on the metal door softly and waited. He could hear the sound of a television, so he rapped much harder, so hard in fact he could hear the insulation on both sides of the door settle.

Max Cameron had an enormous chest. There was a patch of hair from armpit to armpit like a narrow rug. His hands and face and neck were all leathery and creased from working underground, yet his arms and belly were the color of milk.

"I'm Joe," he said. "I came for Mary."

"I can see who you are," said Max, talking through the screendoor. "What do you want with her?"

"Nothing," said Joe. "She's invited for dinner. That's all."

"Amgold is here for you," Max Cameron yelled, his gravel voice filling the trailer.

Before Joe backed off onto the trailer's deck, he saw that the small kitchen sink was piled with dishes and that there were clothes and magazines lying about everywhere. He heard a toilet almost flush.

"I like those flies you tied. I've had good luck with them," Joe said. "When would you like me to bring Mary home?"

But Max was no longer interested in Joe.

"Mary Lee," he said in that same harsh voice, "you be home by ten. Do you hear?"

As if she were imitating her father, she replied with the same harsh meanness, "I hear you!"

Then they were outside and she was standing close to him. He could smell the perfume she had on, and from beneath her white hat her long blonde hair fell over her blouse.

"Hey, come on, let's get out of here," she said.

She did not bother to say good-bye to her father, but then he had disappeared into the depths of the long dim trailer, wandering back through the tunnellike darkness to the television set.

They took a shortcut through Flame's corral, climbed the fence, and walked down Route 24 following the river downstream toward the plank bridge.

Mary was sort of shy and quiet with him. She kept patting her hair and hiking up her jeans.

As they walked, Joe watched the river move away from them faster than they were walking. "Was your father angry or something?" Joe finally asked her.

His words seemed to bring her out of a dream. "Oh, him!" she said. "He's always like that, especially when he's had to stay in the store all day. Well, he's not always like that." Then, she shook out her hair again. "Oh, yes he is. He's always like that, he's like that to everyone. He has to be a little nicer when he's at the store or he wouldn't have any customers at all. I don't like him very much." She twisted away from Joe and ran a few steps ahead. "Oh, what do you care about it!" she said.

"He's your father," said Joe. "He was nice to me in the store."

"Your father's like that, I bet," she said.

"Nice at work and nasty at home," Joe said quickly. "No, he's not. Not usually."

He found himself walking slower now and not wanting to catch up with her and her bad mood. Something was wrong. She wasn't acting the same with him. Rather than lose her completely, he ran and took her hand in his as they were crossing the plank bridge.

"It's too narrow to hold hands," said Mary. She shook off his hand and walked ahead.

They were in dusk now, with no lights. She stopped and faced him.

"Did you tell?" she asked.

"What?"

"Did you tell about my pa in the mine up there?"

"No. I wouldn't."

"I don't believe you."

"Why not? I didn't. I promise I didn't."

"Because he knows your father knows, that's why. And he's mad at me," said Mary. "He thinks it's my fault."

Joe searched for some way to make her anger leave her. "Mary, I did not break my promise," he said. "I can't."

The road up to the house was not too narrow for them to walk side-by-side. They had walked on it before holding hands, but she would not take his until they were almost up to the house, and she took his hand then only because she was scared.

She marched up the porch steps, and all Joe could hope was that his mother and father wouldn't notice her stuffy nose and red eyes.

Mary was off to do a job and she was determined to do it, that was all. Joe knew that, but what he didn't know then was that she was doing all of this for him.

Her boots sounded like bullets on the porch steps.

"Well, here I am! Now what?" she called, in that cheerful, chatterbox way. "I'm starving!"

The dinner was Joe's favorite. Pork chops on rice with a can of crushed tomatoes poured over the top and baked for an hour or so until the rice was done. His mother had decided the rainbow trout wouldn't feed them all. Since Mr. Robbins couldn't eat onions, there were none. The only spices his mother used were sage and pepper, scattered over the braised pork chops.

"This is my all-time favorite," Joe said. That was true.

"We never have this," said Mary. "It's different." She was only picking at her food, though she liked it, because she had eaten earlier with Max when he got home from the store. She forced as much down as she could, but it was hard, because she wasn't hungry to begin with. She was hiding pieces of pork under her pile of rice.

Mr. and Mrs. Robbins sat at either end of the long dining room table. Mary and Joe were facing each other. The large table made Joe feel as if they were all at a meeting, rather than having dinner together. There was a tablecloth and candles and the table seemed longer than it usually was. Perhaps his mother had added a leaf to make their meal seem more like a celebration. Well, it had the opposite effect on Joe.

"My son tells me that you ride, Miss Cameron," his father said from far down the table.

No one heard Mary's response, because she looked at her plate when she spoke, and she didn't seem to be at all excited about her riding, not even in the Cheyenne Days Parade as one of the Queen's attendants. Joe knew that she was terribly happy that she and Flame were going to be in the parade and that she was looking forward to that event more than anything. But her face was pale and she couldn't eat.

"May I please be excused," she said. "I don't feel too well."

Mr. Robbins motioned for Joe to remain seated as they watched Mary dash from the room and run outside. When they heard her being sick on the lawn, Joe's father said, "I'd better call Cameron and have him take her home." Joe's mother went outside to help Mary, leaving Joe alone at the enormous dining room table. He listened to his father talking to Max Cameron. "I don't think it's serious," Mr. Robbins said, "just a nervous stomach is all. You might want to come and get her."

When Cameron's truck came up the road, Joe left the table and watched from the living room window. Something told him not to go to her. So he watched. Mary had not finished being sick and his mother held her as she bent over the porch railing. Max Cameron did not get out of his truck, nor did he turn off the headlights.

"That's too bad," said Mr. Robbins, who now stood next to Joe. "She seemed like such a polite girl."

Mary threw up again on the road as his mother helped her walk toward Cameron's truck.

When Joe moved to go to Mary, his father held his arm.

"Let your mother take care of it," he said. "She is probably very embarrassed."

Joe watched Mary climb into the truck.

Then a strange thing happened. One of them, either

Max or Mary, honked the truck's horn. It was one of those air-powered horns that plays a little melody. The tune from the horn sounded over and over again.

"That's typical of a man like Cameron," said Joe's father.

However, Joe knew, though he didn't say anything, he knew in his bones that it was Mary who was doing the honking and that she was doing it with her father's approval and that she was doing it to get even with all of them. Even when the noise was far down the road, Joe heard that horn blasting in his mind, playing its little tune to make fun of him.

There was cherry cobbler for dessert, made from cherries his mother had picked from the tree in the backyard, but Joe asked if he could be excused. He went down the road to the Arkansas and threw rocks into his fishing pool until the mosquitoes became too thick. By the time he made his way back to the house, his hands and face were covered with welts, the poison was especially severe around his cut, but he didn't care. He didn't care about anything anymore. He had lost her, and now he could not feel even the memory of her lips and tongue along his cheek.

# CHAPTER 15

For the next few days he stayed in bed for as long as he could each morning. It would be raining sometimes and he'd hear Max Cameron blasting away in his tunnel. If it were sunny, he'd sit up every now and then to look out of his tower window to see if Mary had spread out the white towel on the mine dump. He looked for the signal, but knew it would not be there. Not ever, not ever again.

When his mother urged him out of the house, Joe went immediately up to their secret place, to The Tub behind the shaft house, hoping she might be there, even though she hadn't signaled for him.

He climbed onto the tin roof of the shaft house and watched the highway below, waiting for her to appear on Flame. He could see Stringtown from where he was perched. He could see Flame in his corral. He could see

Max's turquoise pickup truck parked at the Granite Store. He knew it was hopeless, for he knew she could see him sitting on the roof of the shaft house. She could come up there. No one was there on sunny days. There was no danger. The heat on the tin roof warmed his clothes and boots. It was peaceful up there.

In the late afternoon, or sometimes during the night, the usual thunderstorm passed down the Arkansas Valley going from Leadville through Granite and out onto the eastern slope of the Rockies, heading for Kansas. Joe learned to time the thundershowers, learning just when they would end. And he would walk up the hillside to the old mine and smell the fresh sage in the air. He would collect wildflowers as he climbed the hill—it seemed like a small hill now, he'd climbed the mountainside so often that summer—and put the flowers in a plastic bag which he would later transfer into his flower press. It was something to do. The fishing was interesting, but Mary would never look for him at the riverbank. It was too public with all the trucks and cars going by all the time. Besides, her father had a view of the road from the store. If she wanted to see him, she would meet him at The Tub. That was that. It was their place. It was their private place.

Of course, she never came to him. Yet, he kept his hopes up. He had nothing else but hope and the memory of the way she had touched him that made him understand that his face was not ugly, that he was not ugly.

The mark on his face had changed in the past few weeks. It was not as swollen and pink as it had been, but had reduced itself to a brilliant red line, less massive but more obvious. The marks from the stitches had been absorbed by his flesh, but that thin red line on his cheek remained. He could touch it himself now without wincing. He would trace his finger along the mark with the identical curiosity that Mary had traced it with her tongue weeks before. That mark, from the accident that happened so long ago that summer, no longer frightened him, as it once had. Thanks to Mary's kiss. And he no longer turned that side of his face toward the pillow when his parents wished him good night.

It seemed like years since he had seen Mary.

Flame remained in his corral.

Max's truck was parked at the Granite Store.

Joe made his daily, midmorning hike up to the mine.

Mary was not around.

The grass in The Tub was not matted down any longer, from their lying there.

Once, Joe awoke in the middle of the night to find that his tower room was surrounded entirely by clouds and, though it was not raining, the sky was alive with dry-lightning. The bolts cracked and sizzled like crazy around the house. But it was not raining. There was no sound of Max working in the tunnel. It was just a cloud around the house pierced by shots of lightning like fire bolts. Joe got out of bed and watched perhaps ten lightning bolts strike the ground just beyond the porch. The sky became lighted, every now and again, with veins of fire. That massive thunderhead would pass on down the valley and leave its moisture somewhere to the southwest over Buena Vista or La Junta.

He went back to bed.

In the morning, he saw the white up on the hillside by the shaft house, and thought it was Mary's signal. It was by sheer chance that Joe was looking out of his window at the same moment the shaft house, the tunnel entrance, and The Tub all turned white and then yellow.

The noise from the explosion did not reach the house until the yellow flame was far off the hillside, like a bright balloon. Joe watched as the pieces from the shaft house settled lower down the hill below the mine dump. A sheet of tin was picked up by the current of hot air and sailed toward the Arkansas River. Then, the noise of the explosion came and all the windows rattled in his tower room.

Smoke billowed continuously from where the shaft house had stood. All that was left on the side of the mountain above the mine dump was a dark opening, a horrid scar on the hillside. Once the noise had passed, once the yellow flames had drifted south, all that was left was a smoldering pile of ruin. Slabs of pine lying everywhere.

Joe had seen it all. It took him some time to realize that it was not lightning that struck the tin roof of the shaft house. A few moments later, a far more familiar sound occurred, that deep rumbling of dynamite inside the mountain that Joe had learned to recognize.

His mother had opened the trapdoor to Joe's room and was next to him now.

"That wasn't thunder," he said to her.

"It wasn't?"

"No." Then, he told her about the box of dynamite he

had seen the first and the only time he had been in the old mine. "I think that's what happened," Joe said. "Because of the storm and all."

Then they both heard the thud of yet another dynamite blast.

"He's in the tunnel," Joe said. "Max is up there in the tunnel. He always works in bad weather. I bet he's trapped in there."

"We should call your father," she said.

They were downstairs and Mrs. Robbins had reached her husband via a radio connection to the Jeep when Joe saw Mary running up their road.

Her white Levi's were dirty and her hair was all over the place and her shirt was ripped up the side. When he let her inside, he saw her face was a mess, covered with dirt and ashes and tear stains.

Joe's mother embraced Mary until she had settled down enough to tell them what had happened.

He had been right. What Joe had seen happen was the shaft house exploding, causing the mine entrance and part of the tunnel to collapse.

"He's inside, my father is trapped in the tunnel!" she cried, becoming hysterical again. "I tried to get him out. I tried!"

When Joe's father arrived, she told him what had happened.

At once Mr. Robbins understood. "Rotten dynamite," he said, "set off by the storm." He sent Joe's mother down to the Granite Store for help.

Joe and Mary and Mr. Robbins went up to the gash in

the side of the mountain. The explosion had picked up the shaft house and what remained of it was a pile of rubble scattered over the mine dump. The box stove was dented like a tin can and the mattress from the bunk was a smoldering ruin. Tools and pieces of bent metal were scattered around the entrance to the mine. The door to the tunnel entrance had vanished and beams hung every which way, blocking the hole in the side of the mountain.

Mary rushed to the entrance and called for her father. After yelling herself nearly hoarse, they all heard a faint voice.

"He's alive," she said. "He's still alive. I just know he is."

Mr. Robbins pulled Mary away from the entrance in fear that the tunnel entrance would collapse even further. A cloud of smoke drifted over them, forcing them all away from the ruined mine.

"Don't worry," Mr. Robbins said to Mary. "We will do something."

Joe left them and went around the entrance and up to The Tub. Their secret place was now sunk into the shape of a small volcano with a gaping hole in the center of it. The grass and trees had been torn from their roots, exposing the bare rock under the thin topsoil. Aspen trees lay in a jumble over the crater's mouth like fallen matchsticks.

Then Joe returned to his father and Mary. They were at a distance from the shattered entrance to the mine. Beams and boulders were strewn in the tunnel, making entering nearly impossible.

"We have to save him!" Mary cried. "We just have to."

It wasn't Max Joe was thinking about, but Mary, when he said, "I'll go in. I will."

His father was going to protest, but the entrance was too small for him to go in. Only Joe would fit.

"Take a bar with you and bar down as you move forward," said his father. "Bar down the tunnel as you go like I showed you."

While Mr. Robbins cared for Mary, Joe began the slow process of tapping all the beams and boulders above the entrance. Rocks and dirt cascaded to his feet. He ducked under a beam and squeezed into the tunnel, crawling, wedging his way inside. A side of the tunnel wall looked as if it were swollen and Joe used the bar. A virtual landslide of loose rock swept in front of him as if a truck had dumped a load at his feet. What had happened was that the explosion and Joe's bar had opened an old air shaft that Max had filled with waste rock to keep his working the mine a secret. That loose fill now blocked the tunnel entirely and it would take hours to clear the passage.

Carefully, Joe backed out of the tunnel and into the daylight.

"Take your time," his father called to him. "Are you hurt?"

"No," Joe said, "but I can't get through. It's caved in."

"You did the right thing," said his father. "You probably saved your life." Then Mr. Robbins said to Mary, "How long has he been in there?"

"Maybe two hours," she said.

"We have to find another way," said Joe's father.

# CHAPTER 16

"There's a hole up above," said Joe. "I can go down that way."

Joe took them up to the place where The Tub had been.

"Hello, hello," Mary yelled into the crater. "Daddy, can you hear me?"

Immediately, Max Cameron responded. They couldn't hear exactly what he said, but his voice was much louder than it had been when they heard it from the tunnel entrance.

Max's voice became stronger. "I can see daylight," he said. "I can't move. My legs are trapped."

"We have to get a rope on him," said Mr. Robbins.

Before his father could stop him, Joe was sliding down

the steep walls of the crater using the fallen trees to hold him back. Grass and topsoil and rocks disappeared in the sinkhole. A tree had fallen across the crater's opening and Joe crawled onto it and lowered himself until he was hanging over the dark opening. He moved, hand over hand, along the branch until it bent and gently lowered him into the darkness.

Joe found himself on a pile of earth. The tunnel disappeared in both directions.

"Max," Joe said softly.

"I'm here. Up ahead."

Joe slid down the pile of slick wet earth and moved toward the voice in the darkness.

"Keep coming," Max said. "I can see you now."

He found Max Cameron buried up to his waist in heavy muck. One of his legs was trapped. It took some time for Joe to push away the heavy rock, flinging mud and rocks into the darkness.

"Easy, easy," said Max in his gravel voice, "I'm not going anywhere. My leg's busted."

Joe could hear the voices of those above him, but he couldn't understand what they said.

"I found him," Joe yelled.

One of them, probably Mary, must have tried to slide down the steep side of the crater, for suddenly a massive hunk of earth broke from the tunnel ceiling only a few feet from Joe and Max.

The light in the tunnel became brighter with the opening of the hole.

"Stay back," Joe called. "I can do it."

Max was free now and Joe pulled him toward the opening and up the slick pile of earth trying to get them both into a position so that there was blue sky over their heads. Another hunk of the tunnel ceiling fell, grazing Joe's shoulder, tearing his shirt.

Joe did not have the strength to carry Max up the mound of earth, so he crawled forward and pulled him by his coat while Max pushed with his good leg. The torrent of swearing and cussing that came from the injured man was like something Joe had never heard before.

Joe's mother and a few men had arrived by this time. One of the men tossed the end of a rope down to Joe and told him how to tie a sling around Max. They were on the top of the earth mound now and free from falling earth.

Getting Max out of that crater opening was like getting someone out of a hole in ice. Each time the men pulled Max to the crater's lip, four or five truckloads of earth fell into the tunnel. Joe stayed close to Max, pushing, as he was lifted out.

Max was lying on solid ground now and, in his hurry to get out, he stepped on Joe's head, mashing his face against a chunk of sharp granite. Joe felt the old wound on his face being pressed into the rock, but Max continued to try and free himself. Joe's face was mashed against the sharp rock, grating and rubbing against it as Max struggled.

Then Max was out of the tunnel and the end of the rope appeared for him. Without bothering to make a sling, Joe held on and was pulled from the gaping mouth of the sinkhole.

**115**

"Mary!" he called.

But the men from Granite were now halfway down the mountainside carrying Max and Mary was with them. Far down the hillside on the road an ambulance waited to take Max away.

"Let her go," said Joe's father. He handed Joe a handkerchief and told him to press it to his face.

"What about Mary," he asked, "and Max?"

His father put his hand on his shoulder. "Joe, try and forget them. It hurts, but try."

"You did a brave thing," his mother said.

"No!" said Joe. "It was stupid. Anyone could have done it. Anyone. Mary, even."

"But you did," his mother said. "And you're going to be fine."

They let him rest by himself on the mine dump.

After a while, his father said, "I think we'd better go down to the house and get a bandage for that cheek of yours. It's just a nick."

"Do you hurt anywhere?" his mother asked.

"Yes. A little. Here." But he couldn't find the exact spot. "It's somewhere around here," he said, patting the front of his shoulder where his shirt had been torn by the falling rock.

# CHAPTER 17

By the time Joe left Granite that summer, his cut cheek no longer hurt him. His shoulder had been bruised, not broken. He was thankful it was his left shoulder and not his right, so he was able to go fishing a few more times before they packed up to leave for Towlesport.

Even after he had been home and had been attending school for a few weeks, the scar on his face reminded him of Mary Cameron. He stayed in the bathroom each morning longer than necessary looking in the mirror. He wondered if Mary still rode Flame. He wondered if she was in the Cheyenne Days Parade with her father. He wondered if Max Cameron was still tying Humphys and working in the mine. Max's broken leg would be healed by now.

All he told his classmates about what had happened to him that summer was that he had hurt himself and that it was an accident. He kept the rest to himself. And he kept his scar covered with gauze.

"It was nobody's fault," he said to Bertie Feather one day. "It just happened."

They were alone in the front of Mr. Feather's Corner Store.

"Won't it go away sometime?" she asked. "When will you take the gauze off?"

When she reached out to touch Joe's cheek, he backed away.

"Come on, Joe," she said. "It can't be that bad-looking. Besides, I like your eyes. That's what I like."

She teased him in a way that made him feel warm.

Still, Joe kept his scar covered. It was not necessary. Yet, he went to school with a fresh piece of gauze on his face each morning.

If he seemed to be lost during the first months of school that year, it was not because he was hiding his scar. It was because he missed Mary Cameron.

He had only two things to remember her by. He had the cut, which he kept hidden from the world. And he had the cherry pit she had given to him, which was wrapped in white tissue paper and hidden in the leather-covered box in the top right-hand drawer of his blue bureau under his socks.

He no longer walked to school with Roy Boland and Bill Hymes. Instead, he left his house early and went to the Corner Store to wait until Bertie Feather was finished with her morning's work.

He liked the mornings there. The waitress behind the counter was full of jokes and laughed easily. She slid enormous platters of eggs and sausages and Mr. Feather's homefries down the counter. "Three scrambled with sausage for John," the waitress would say as she let the platter go. The plumber, Billy Waters, lifted his coffee cup to take a sip, and the plate of food slid right past him. Then Billy would look down the counter and see that the platter had stopped directly in front of John Barron, the animal doctor. Then Billy would put his coffee cup back down on the counter at exactly the same moment his plate of French toast and bacon arrived, clinking against his coffee cup.

"Doughnut Bertie" worked the cash register and handled the take-out orders until it was time for school. Her new whole-wheat-and-blueberry recipe was not too popular, but the cinnamon-raisin was. She tended to keep the powdered doughnuts out of sight, so she could have them for herself after school.

For her first report in Mr. Gadd's social studies class, Bertie had brought in about fourteen different kinds of doughnuts she had invented during the summer. Most of Joe's classmates brought in photographs of where they had been. There was Bill Hymes in the lifeguard chair at Plum Island and a few snapshots of him in a small sailboat;

**119**

there were Roy Boland's pictures of Towlesport from a rented airplane that showed the roof of his house; there was Rebecca Majors holding a trophy for rollerskating in Camden, Maine.

Joe's report consisted of a miniature gold recovery machine, which his father helped him build. It was made of an old rock polisher that ran on an electric motor and a dishpan with a tube coming out of the bottom and metal riffles riveted to the sides. His father had given him some high-grade ore, maybe a cupful, and helped Joe put a fan in the porcelain dish. Before the class, Joe showed how the rock was pulverized. He added the chemicals to make a slurry and poured it into the pan. Gradually the water cleared as the fan blades forced the waste into the riffles on the side. Then he took the cork out of the tube. What filled the milk bottle looked dark and murky at first, then it settled. There was some sand mixed in with the quartz, but at the very bottom was a dark layer of microscopic particles of gold. "And, that's my summer," he said.

"How much gold is that?" someone asked, probably Bill Hymes.

"Once it's refined and melted down," said Joe, "it would make a nugget the size of a pencil eraser. At least, that's what my father estimated."

"How did you hurt yourself?" asked Rebecca Majors, who had a sprained ankle from her last roller-skating meet in Concord, New Hampshire.

"It was an accident," Joe said. "It was no one's fault."

That day after school, Bertie Feather helped Joe carry

his miniature gold recovery invention home. Everyone had eaten her doughnuts, so her arms were free.

"What *did* happen to your cheek?" she said. "Let me see."

They were in his garage putting the equipment away.

Bertie moved closer to Joe. Then she touched the side of his face, moving her fingers over the gauze. "You shouldn't be ashamed," she said.

"I'm not!" The anger in Joe's voice surprised him. "I am not ashamed of it."

He wanted her to leave. He wanted to run into the house to his room. He wanted to call Mary at the Granite Store. He could get her telephone number easily. And if she wasn't there, she would get off the couch from in front of the television and answer the phone in her trailer in Stringtown. If she didn't answer the telephone, then that meant she was riding Flame in a parade somewhere. Mary was swimming in his memory now, yet it was Bertie Feather who was holding his hand.

"Come on, Joe. Come closer," Bertie said.

She let go of his hand and touched his bandage.

"Now," she said, "let's see what you have been hiding."

Her voice was as gentle as her touch. She was kind and soft and curious. Her voice was warm like hot sand when you are alone with no one else around for miles and you are in the little valley the wind makes between two sand dunes with the ocean and the wind in your ears. "That's it," said Bertie. "Don't move."

Her fingers on his cheek were like a soft pool of light.

He felt her dark hair touch his arm. Her touch made him feel dizzy.

She pulled at the tape. "Does it hurt when I do that?"

"No. It just hurts a little when I wash my face in water that's too hot. Here, let me do it."

Joe peeled off the bandage. She looked at his scar and shook her head.

Joe expected her to flinch and look away, but Bertie's eyes remained soft and kind. "I don't think I'll wear this anymore," he said.

Then she touched his scar, and her finger was like a feather on his cheek.

"Will you walk me home now?" she asked. Joe nodded. He saw his bandage lying on the tool shelf. He picked it up and tossed it into the pile of empty oil cans and trash. They left the garage together and walked outside into the afternoon sunlight.